Happy new

Very best wishes

Clare Cassy :)

The Bed & Breakfast Queen

CLARE CASSY

First published in Great Britain 2018
©2018 Clare Cassy

For my Mother Sheila, the original 'B&B Queen,' who found Willow Cottage and my Brother Stu, who loved the house.

Remembered with a smile.

ACKNOWLEDGEMENTS

Huge thanks again, to Martin for his infinite patience, excellent
editing skills and wonderful cover.
A thank you too, to my dear young friend, Apratim
for his advice on choosing Holly's car.
Special days together watching 'Top Gear.'

Cover Design and layout: illuminati-design.co.uk

THE BED & BREAKFAST QUEEN

Chapter One

"What? You're going to give everything up to run a Bed and Breakfast in the back of beyond? You can't be serious?" Mac scoffed, as Holly was stirring a bolognaise sauce that evening. "You're clearly in line to be editor, Hol. You must be mad... Burying yourself in the country, slaving over a pan of bacon and eggs... tripping over bundles of dirty washing!"

Holly sighed. She was losing him. His body language said it all. At one time, he would have his arms around her waist, nuzzling her neck as she was cooking. But now he was coming home later and later from the office.

"I'm tired of chasing scummy stories and persuading people to sell their souls for a few hundred quid Mac... Yes, it's been fun and I love everybody I work with on the magazine but I am tired. I've done it since I was nineteen and now I've turned thirty, I want to do something else. It's a fantastic property, at a knock down price, it could be a new start for us both."

Holly looked at him with hope in her eyes as she re-filled their wine glasses.

"Just come and see it with me. Please Mac?"

Mac pushed his thick mop of blond hair back from his face as he went through the motions of looking at the property details Holly had laid out on their stainless-steel kitchen worktop.

It was obvious he wasn't interested in going to see it with her. Holly sighed sadly as she turned her attention to serving their food. They ate in silence. An awkward, heavy presence hanging in the air.

Both worked hard and were successful in their respective careers. He was Creative Director of one of the most successful advertising agencies in London, while Holly was Features Editor for a well-known women's weekly magazine. They went away for weekends to Paris, Florence, Barcelona and Rome. Ate at the best restaurants. Drank in all the well-known media drinking bars. Life had been good until Holly accidently became pregnant.

It was a shock to them both as she'd been having regular contraceptive injections for the past three years and had never missed an appointment for a top-up treatment. Until last month. Mac was furious and blamed her for their predicament.

"How could you have been so irresponsible? he'd shouted at her, that awful night in the restaurant. Didn't you note down the date of your appointment? How the hell could you have missed it?"

"I had a deadline Mac and couldn't leave the office. Work took over and I just forgot to go. I didn't do it on purpose if that's what you are thinking."

"I don't know what to think," he'd hissed at her. The sad thing was that she'd been so excited when the line turned blue on the pregnancy test and was sure he would come around; after all it wasn't as if they were in the first flush of youth, they were financially secure – living in Mac's spacious, ultra-modern, high tech apartment in London's fashionable East End and had been together for five good years.

"Things worked out for Abigail and Pete," Holly added in a softer tone. "Look how devastated he was when she told him she was pregnant."

"True, now he's an even bigger baby bore than she is. Don't you remember that awful night we went out with them and all they talked about was liquidizing baby food? I'm sorry Holly, I'm just not ready to be a father." Avoiding her eyes and fiddling nervously with the cutlery in front of him, it was clear that the subject wasn't up for further discussion.

"So, I'm good enough to sleep with for five years but not good enough to have your child... is that it?" She was starting to shout and Mac was looking mortified as the couple on the next table were clearly ear-wigging.

"If this child was the result of a one night stand I could understand Mac."
Unable to bare his callous attitude any longer, her eyes had filled with tears as she flung down her napkin, marched out the restaurant and hailed a cab home.

"You alright luv?" The kindly cabbie had asked.

"Yes, fine thanks," she stammered, choking back huge, thick sobs that strangled her voice. Then to her amazement she told him everything.

"Don't worry, he'll come 'round luv, that's men for ya. See these?" he said, proudly pointing out five or six pictures of children of various ages pinned around the inside of his cab, "They're me pride and joy, all five of 'em. But when the missus told me she was first expectin' I thought me world 'ad come to an end. You'll see luv, he'll come 'round. Five years you've been together? Course 'e will..."

But Mac didn't. When he came back later that night they slept as far apart from each other as they could. He undressed in silence as Holly sobbed into the sheets. The silence between them was deafening and two weeks later, she had a miscarriage. Mac was foul and his distant and uncaring attitude to her distress was proving to be the death knoll for their relationship.

But someone or something, was tweaking Holly's destiny.

She was recovering at home when her mother rang.

"Holly darling, I have a letter for you. Looks like it is from Auntie Maud. Shall I forward it, or will you get it when you come down?" she asked hopefully.
Holly wasn't in the best frame of mind to visit her parents. She was so miserable she could hardly bear her own company let alone be around anyone else.

"Do you mind reading it to me Mum?"
There was a rustle of paper as her mother opened the letter.

"God, her writing. I can barely read it... right..."
Holly's mother took a deep breath.

Dearest, darling Holly,
I don't think I have long for this world. Don't be sad, I have spent too long on this earth.

"Oh, my goodness," Holly's mum gulped...
I would like you to buy yourself a house with whatever is left of my estate once the nursing home where I have resided these last few years has been paid. Your mother and father worry about you, as do I.
Get out of London dear. Buy yourself a house in a proper part of England. Somewhere where the air is fresh and you can find yourself a good man, who will love and cherish you and your children. Don't leave it too late like your old Auntie Maud.
I have instructed my solicitor accordingly.

Your loving,
Great Auntie Maud

"Oh my God Mum!" Holly burst into tears.

"Dear, Oh, dearie me," her mother repeated in between sobs. It was a full five minutes before either of them could draw breath. It was as if the old lady knew what had happened between Holly and Mac.

But she couldn't possibly have known because Holly hadn't even told her mother about her miscarriage.

The day after they received her letter, Auntie Maud died a spinster. Colin, her childhood sweetheart, who she called out for on her deathbed, was killed in the Second World War. Shot down with his crew in their Lancaster bomber, somewhere over Germany. He'd just turned eighteen and was the rear gunner. He'd lied about his age to join the Air Force.

"No one could match Colin," Auntie Maud would say, adding wistfully, "Besides, after the war there weren't enough men left to go around. I wasn't the only girl never to get married. There was a whole bunch of us."

So she ended her days in a nursing home in Eastbourne after a life looking after other people's children. Holly had many happy memories of spending time with her. Looking at faded old photos of Colin; baking or sewing in her house which smelt of cats and mothballs.

"Auntie Maud would have been a wonderful mother," Holly's mother used to say, "She just had that way with children."

She gave Holly the letter at the old lady's funeral and Holly re-read the feminine, spidery handwriting at her graveside.

"Thank you, Auntie Maud," she whispered, placing Colin's photo and a bouquet of violets - her auntie's favourite flowers, on her grave. She could picture her in her bed at the nursing home; propped up like a little bird in her nest of white pillows; clad in a pink, winceyette nightie, her long, thin, grey hair neatly styled into a bun at the nape of her neck. The faded photograph of her beloved Colin, on her bedside table. Life could be so cruel, Holly reflected sadly; so many of Auntie Maud's generation were denied the chance of marriage and a normal, family life, as were a lot of women in Holly's generation now; albeit in a different way because Holly wasn't the only one of her friends, itching to hang up her corporate suit and have a baby. Then, when and if they became a mother, they had to rush back to work to pay the mortgage with constant feelings of guilt that they couldn't spend more time at home. Women like her friend Maggie, who was dreading going back to the job she hated after the birth of her baby, but had no choice. Maggie's husband had also made it very clear that they could never afford to have another child either.

"I'd have loved to have had more children," Maggie had said, wistfully, adding: "What I'd do to stay at home and make playdoh and jam tarts."

In many ways, Holly's mother and her generation who married and had children in the 1950's didn't know how lucky they were. As much as Mum moaned about having to be a 'stay-at-home mother,' she never battled with the exhaustion and guilt that so many of Holly's generation of young working mothers faced every day.

Maybe the old lady was right and Holly would be happier in a 'Proper part of England,' the idea of moving out of London and finding a husband who could cherish her and their baby would be wonderful.

Yes, Auntie Maud, I am going to leave London and start a new life, somewhere where the air is fresh and clean… Rest in peace, with your Colin.

Holly was just reading the cards on the flowers when her mother came hobbling over in her high heels, dramatically holding on to her hat.

"Holly darling, there you are. We're making our way to the hotel for drinks. Dad's just getting the car," she said, getting all motherly and linking arms with her only daughter. "You are looking a bit peaky dear."

"I'm alright." Holly lied.

"Good, now you must talk to your cousin Grace. Did I tell you she's pregnant? My sister's going to be a grandmother! I always thought it would be me first." she sighed, holding tighter on to Holly's arm.

Chapter Two

'You have reached your destination.'
Thank God for my Sat Nav, Holly mused as she saw the impressive iron, black and white Bed and Breakfast sign gently swaying in the West Sussex wind. She'd never been any good at reading maps and was sure she wouldn't have found her way without it.

Indicating left as directed, she drove slowly down the long, sweeping, tree-lined driveway into the *'Willow Cottage Bed and Breakfast'* establishment. Her car tyres slowly crunching over the pearl-grey coloured gravel. Then, carefully parking her pink Volkswagen Beetle and switching off the engine, she checked her hair in the car's mirror, put a dab of powder on her nose and re-newed her trade-mark, cherry red lipstick. Not bad timing; she'd driven down from London in just over an hour and a half and was five minutes early for her appointment with Mrs Baxter, the vendor.

The word 'Cottage' was misleading, to say the least, as there were sixteen bedrooms. Built in the classic Elizabethan 'L' shape, it was painted an attractive shade of green. Roses clustered around the door way and Hollyhocks and Delphiniums vied for attention with Lilac, Marigolds, Daisies and Sweet Peas in the long front garden. Oh, this was a real olde-English country-cottage garden.

How clean the air smelt after London, the sky was a bright blue and Holly could swear she hadn't seen such white, fluffy clouds in a very long time. Two sweet, little robins were pecking excitedly at some breadcrumbs scattered on a windowsill.

Holly's high heels sank into the gravel as she made her way down the side of the house to the front entrance.

A massive dog with a very loud, deep bark bounded to the front door as soon as she rang the bell. A moment or so later, it was answered by a small, fresh faced woman carrying a chunky baby. She looked around thirty, the same age as Holly, with unkempt, shoulder length hair. As her eyes scanned Holly, her face dropped. Somehow, she couldn't see such a 'girl about town' in her pencil skirt and tasteful silk blouse turning out plates of eggs and bacon every morning.

Christine Baxter sighed to herself as she invited her in. She was bound to be another time waster, traipsing through the house making infuriating comments about all the improvements she would make.

"Miss Bradbury?"

"Yes, that's me," Holly answered brightly.

"And you must be Mrs Baxter?"

"I am. And this is Tess," she said wearily, indicating the dog, to assure Holly it wouldn't eat her for breakfast.

"Her bark is a lot worse than her bite, don't worry." *Thank God for that*, thought Holly. She liked dogs but this one was huge – an English Bullmastiff apparently, and she wouldn't want to get on the wrong side of it.

"Your baby is lovely, how old is he?... She?"

"He. Bobby, five months." Mrs Baxter answered proudly, jiggling him on her hip. He was so perfect with his little rosebud mouth and shock of dark hair. Holly's breath was momentarily taken away as she felt a surge of longing, crossed with a familiar, stabbing loss. *What would our baby have looked like at this age?* She would have liked to have held little Bobby but Mrs Baxter kept him protectively tucked under her ample arm.

Tapestries and pictures of various country scenes adorned the walls of the entrance hall. A small table by the front-door was crowded with business cards and tourist guides of every shape and size. Following Mrs

Baxter, baby and dog, Holly made her way past a large kitchen and laundry room into a spacious back sitting room with a very attractive, open brick fireplace.

"Sit yourself down," Mrs Baxter gestured politely, indicating the sofa, the majority of which was immediately swiped by the dog. "Don't mind Tess, she's an asset in a place like this, you never know who is going to turn up at your door."

Still cradling her baby, she explained that they lived in this part of the house while the rest of the property was set-aside for guests. A small bathroom and box-room for the baby led off from the sitting room, while the Baxter's' bedroom and adjoining store room were more modern additions to the house. Holly had the feeling this wasn't going to be a very long tour of the house; Mrs Baxter seemed tired and was obviously pre-occupied with the baby. *Where was her husband? Shouldn't he be showing her around as the poor woman was obviously so exhausted?*

Holly was dying for a coffee but she didn't really blame Mrs Baxter for not offering her one. It couldn't be much fun having people tramp through your house especially when it was so large and you had to lug a chunky baby around.

The kitchen was a million miles from the high-tech minimalist, chrome one Holly and Mac shared in London. Holly loved the long, scrubbed, pine trestle table and matching, impressive dresser, cluttered with brightly coloured china.

A welcoming warmth and smell of baking emanated from the Aga cooker as Mrs Baxter led Holly through to the dining room. About half a dozen little tables sporting yellow and white checked table-clothes were covered with an assortment of stainless-steel teapots and little jugs. *The table cloths would have to go, they must be white linen,* Holly mused.

Used, individual tubs of butter, marmalade and jam were piled in pyramids on empty plates.

"Haven't had a chance to clear up yet what with the little one and all." Mrs Baxter apologised with a soft Sussex burr. The dining room also had a large open fireplace complete with brass bellows, pokers and decorative, iron kettles. An attractive arrangement of dried hops and various brass pans and iron ornaments hung on the walls and a nicely worn Persian carpet added a bit of colour and style to the practical beige carpet. *Nice rug but the carpet's worn and grimy...*

"Guests tell me what time they want breakfast the night before and if they want a 'Full English.' Boiled eggs are the worst," Mrs Baxter smiled, "Some want 'em soft, others 'ard. People gets very fussy about their eggs."

Baby Bobby's eyes studied Holly's face over his mother's shoulder as they left the dining room and mounted the wonderful, sweeping staircase with its wide, shiny, mahogany banister to the bedrooms. There'd be no need for Pilates classes after a daily workout like this. Suddenly, Mrs Baxter stopped in her tracks and doubled back to a room she had seemingly forgotten.

"Now this be the Dame School," she said, as they stepped into a huge musty smelling room cluttered with stepladders and old paint pots. Apparently, it had been added to the house in the latter part of the nineteenth century.

"Them that could afford it, paid a penny a week to 'ave their kiddies learn to read and write and there be the picture to prove it," Mrs Baxter gushed, pointing to a faded old photograph hanging perilously on the wall by a rusty nail.

"That there, be the dame, their teacher, a Miss Gibbons I'm told."

Spellbound, Holly studied the faces of the ragged looking little Victorian children, standing to attention next to the fierce old woman who was clad entirely in black save for her white bonnet.

"Buried in the churchyard, she is… and probably along with some of them little nippers as well." Reluctantly, Holly tore herself away from the picture as Mrs Baxter called her over to a door, which opened out to an outside staircase. Its crumbling, moss-covered, steps descending right down to the back garden.

"See that there oak tree? The family that owned this 'ouse hid King Charles in it when he was fleeing from them Roundheads…"

How could Mrs Baxter bear to leave this house? It was wonderful.

The baby was starting to get a bit tetchy and Holly sensed his mother wanted to get the rest of the viewing over.

The bedrooms on the next two floors were named after flowers. There was the pink 'Wallflower Room,' the blue 'Delphinium', white 'Heliotrope' and the mauve 'Lilac Room.' And that was just for starters. Holly's favourite was the yellow 'Primrose Room' at the top of the house with its sloping ceiling, charming window seat and pretty, stained-glass window.

Um, maybe that could be mine… All had their own little sinks, television and tea and coffee making facilities. *I'll have to invest in new bed linen, Holly mused. People don't like sleeping in flowery bed sheets any more. It had to be white, crisp Egyptian cotton… and the televisions looked a bit old fashioned as well. Everyone expected flat screen, wall mounted TVs now.*

"Now this be our Honeymoon suite," Mrs Baxter laughed, a twinkle in her eye, as they walked up to the third floor.

"It's lovely." Holly remarked truthfully, eyeing the Victorian style cherub above the huge four-poster bed and nicely faded tapestries adorning the walls.

"You have to watch wedding parties tho," Mrs Baxter added, "They can get a bit boisterous sometimes! The last lot smashed all me champagne glasses. Nice little money earners tho'... right, I'll show you the Brewery next," she said, shifting baby Bobby on her hip.

"Oh, that sounds interesting." Holly said brightly, following her gingerly, down a perilous, creaky little staircase.

The Brewery, Mrs Baxter explained, was the oldest part of the house. It had originally been a coaching inn and this was where the horses were rested and beer was served to passing travellers. An attractive modern-day mural of Tudor wenches pouring beer inside a rowdy inn, with boys brushing horses and feeding dogs outside, was painted on one of the walls in the little entrance hall...

"My friend's daughter, painted that when she was fresh out of art school." Mrs Baxter said proudly. It was exquisite.

Holly was enthralled as Mrs. Baxter pulled back the corner of an old Persian rug revealing a rusty metal plate embedded in the floor.

"There's a secret tunnel under 'ere," she said, tapping it with her foot, "Goes straight out to Fishbourne Creek it does... used by boot-leggin pirates doin' their business right 'ere in this brewery with the inn-keeper."

"Oh my god, have you been down there?"

"My hubby tried. Was a helluva job getting this lid off, but the 'ole had all closed up... 'e did a bit a diggin' - mess everywhere there was, but he soon gave up."

Holly could just picture a bunch of rag-tag, Johnny Depp, look-alike, pirates jumping up and out of the tunnel. They probably stood right where she and Mrs Baxter were now. All wiping sweaty brows after the exertions of rolling and heaving up heavy barrels of booze. Candles would be flickering, a mouse scampering here and there along the dusty, flag stones on the brewery floor. The atmosphere would be tense as the inn keeper inspected the barrels. Then after greedily, gulping a beer they'd count the coins they'd been given and beat a hasty retreat down the tunnel to their boats in the harbour.

This house was steeped in history. Holly had never bought a property before but she knew she wanted this one. It had a warm, almost humbling presence and she knew she could be at home here. Forcing herself to go, she thanked Mrs Baxter for her time and said she'd contact the agent to make an offer.
Mrs Baxter didn't look convinced.

"Mac, the house has so much potential. It's all beams and creaky staircases, the bedrooms need updating but with a few changes here and there, it could be a gold mine. There's even a secret tunnel running out to Fishbourne Creek. No wonder it's a favourite with the Americans... You'll love it. Let's talk tonight, I'll be back around seven. Just going to do a little shopping in Chichester..."

Chapter Three

Holly made a supreme effort with dinner that night. She had to win Mac round. She knew she was going to make an offer for the house and wanted him to be part of everything. The wine was nicely chilled and she'd made Mac's favourite dish, spaghetti alle a vongole.

"Look, I understand if you don't want to be involved in the Bed and Breakfast side of things. I can take care of that, you could stay in the flat during the week and come to Chichester at the weekends. You could even work from there a couple of days a week if you wanted?"

"I'm a London boy, Hol. This is your thing."

"But I want it to be our thing. I'm not asking you to give up your job and move down lock, stock and barrel."

Mac was more intent on twirling his pasta expertly around his fork.

"We'll grow apart Hol. You know how it is in my line of work. I have to live and breathe the job, I can't do that if I'm a couple of days here and a couple of days there… Pass that garlic dip."

Holly felt an uncomfortable, gnawing sensation in her stomach. It was decision time.

Holly's editor, Margery Dailey, was predictably, dramatically distraught at Holly's resignation.

"Holly, how are we going to cope without you?" she wailed: "Don't you think you are being a bit hasty? We know you haven't had an easy time recently," she said, obviously referring to Holly's miscarriage, "But this is a bit drastic, isn't it? Have you really thought everything through?"

Holly assured Margery that she had and she was as sure as she could be, that she had made the right decision. She was trading in her killer-heels for green wellies, bumper packs of bacon and a new set of saucepans.

"But darling, you'll be joining the Women's Institute and making jam next." Margery joked.

"Actually, Margery, that's a pretty cool thing to do now, as is learning to knit."

"Oh darling, please, this is getting worse," Margery said in mock horror.

"Think of all those great stories I will be sending you ... 'Stitching and Bitching with the Women's Institute' and 'Falling in love over the breakfast table'..."

Mac rolled his eyes and was momentarily lost for words when Holly told him her offer for the house had been accepted and she'd given in her notice at work. *He didn't think I'd do it.*
They hardly spoke for the next four weeks which Holly found excruciating. Try as she might, she just couldn't get him to take any interest in her new venture.

"He's making me feel like I'm deserting him," she confided miserably to her mother on the phone.

"What will be, will be dear, you've made your decision now. Time will tell. Once you've made the move, and he realises you have gone, he may come around. 'Absence makes the heart grow fonder' as they say, and you, on the other hand, may be quite happy without him..."
For once, Holly had the feeling her mother had really been listening to her.

***

At the end of the month the magazine laid on a wonderful leaving party and to Holly's surprise, Mac even turned up to support her. Champagne flowed at the office and Holly had a hard time bottling up the tears when Margery made her farewell speech.

"Holly darling, we will miss you. Not just us in the office here at '*Smile*' magazine, but all your loyal readers as well. You have a natural nose for a story, your journalistic skills are second to none…" Margery flamboyantly pointed to the framed magazine covers dotted around the office walls with Holly's headlines featured on the covers.

"Wonderful, just wonderful. Spot on every time. Oh dear, I am going to cry," Margery sniffed into her linen hanky. "But we know you will make a success of your new life in the country. We just ask you to keep in touch and maybe do a little freelance writing for us in between cooking all those breakfasts?" And with that, she raised her glass: "Here's to Holly and her new business venture in the country!"

"To Holly and her new business venture in the country!" her colleagues repeated, raising their glasses in unison.

Mac, Holly noticed, hung back, quietly nursing his drink. His smile was set in a tight line as Margery kept pointing out Holly's award-winning stories. Janine, a junior writer then rushed forward with their gifts. A beautiful Tiffany bracelet; a copy of the Women's Institute Cook Book and calendar, and a red and white, fifties-style checked pinny and a rolling pin, 'To chase away any unwelcome guests.'

There was a lump in Holly's throat as she opened them then twirled in the apron brandishing the rolling pin.

"Thank you everybody so much. I miss you all already and yes please, keep in touch. Come and see me, come and stay and yes, yes, send me that freelance writing!" She was about to cry.

"Thank you, Margery," she continued, "For having so much faith in me over the years and being such a wonderful mentor. You are a great editor and I have learnt so much from you. Thank you, Janine for being such fun to work with. You have a fantastic future ahead of you and thank you everyone for making my time here so special. I will miss you all."

The room resounded with applause and even Mac sidled up and slid his arm protectively around her waist. After her third glass of champagne Holly did indeed wonder if she had done the right thing. Could she really see herself cooking eggs and bacon every day? Changing sheets and doing mountains of ironing? Suddenly the thought of vacating her cool office didn't seem such a good idea, and what about her and Mac? They had been good together. She couldn't hold his ambition against him...

"Oh Janine," she cried in the loo, as they renewed their lipstick before heading out to 'Luigis' – a restaurant popular with London's media elite. "Maybe I have been a bit hasty."

"Give it a go Holly, Margery would welcome you back with open arms if things don't work out."

"You think so?"

"I know so." she hugged her friend.

The following week, Holly was shaking hands with Barry, the oily estate agent, as she collected the keys to Willow Cottage.

"A mighty fine load of bricks and mortar you have there, Miss Bradbury," he chuckled, his eyes wandering down to her cleavage. "All the best with your new venture."

"Thank you," Holly answered brightly, almost skipping out of the estate agents.

Well, Aunt Maud, here I am, I hope you would approve,
she mused as she turned the key in the front door.
At the sound of the key in the lock, Tess paddled over
to greet her (Holly had agreed to keep the dog as the
Baxters were down-sizing and being alone in such a big
house, a big scary looking dog like Tess made her feel a
lot safer).

"Hey girl," When Holly bent down to stroke her
behind her ears they were almost the same height.
"Looks like you are my new best friend."

Making her way into the kitchen – new best friend
in tow, she picked up a hand-written note from the
freshly scrubbed kitchen counter. The Baxter's had
vacated the property yesterday but had popped in
earlier to feed Tess and take her out for her last walk
with them.

Holly,
(They were on first name terms now that Holly had
bought the property),
I have taken your first booking.
Edna, from the Millstream Hotel in Bosham (very plush),
rang to say they had an American racing driver booked
in for the next two weeks but they over-booked. He's
competing at the famous Goodwood Races just down the
road. He is staying with you for ten days and wants
breakfast at seven every morning. As he's American and
they like double beds, I've booked him into the
Wallflower Room. Edna often passes bookings on to us
when they are fully booked.
Welcome to Willow Cottage and your new life. Give Tess
a big kiss from us, we will miss her.
All the best
Susan Baxter

Picking up the leather-bound bookings diary the Baxters had left for Holly by the land-line, Holly smiled when she saw that Stuart Perone, was indeed booked in at the beginning of the next week.

"I'd better get cracking getting this place ready old girl," she called over fondly to Tess, who was chewing a tree branch she'd picked up from the fields.

My first guest. Stuart Perone eh? And he's an American racing driver who's coming all the way from New York. Things are looking good.

Making herself a coffee she patted Tess and started to write her 'To Do' list. She got as far as cleaning materials when the phone rang.

"Hello Willow Cottage." she smiled to herself.

"Hi," a cheery female American accent cooed down the phone line. "Is that the proprietor?"

"Er, yes, that's me" Holly answered brightly.

"I am calling from New York for Mr Stuart Perone."

"Oh!" Holly gasped.

"We just wanted to confirm his reservation with you for ten days. The Millstream Hotel, where he usually stays, is fully booked."

"Yes, I heard that," Holly answered, "Don't worry everything is fine here. I will look forward to seeing Mr Perone on Monday the 18th."

"That's great," the voice intoned "We will wire you the cheque straight way."

"Oh goodness, yes." Holly stammered. She didn't know how much she should charge or what happened about wiring a cheque. Talk about being thrown into the deep end.

So, Mrs Baxter had booked him into the Wallflower room.

"C'mon old girl," she called affectionately to Tess. "I'd better go and remind myself where it is."

Heaving herself up from her basket, the dog followed her new mistress obediently up the stairs.

What pleasure Holly felt flinging open the doors to all the rooms - as if to remind herself they really were hers.

Then, when she sat down on one of the beds she thought of Mac. What was he doing now? She wondered wistfully, a tear pricking her eye. What fun it would be to share this new venture. He was a good cook and perhaps they could have branched out into evening meals. She could just see him playing '*Mein Host*' - serving drinks from a little bar. No doubt he'd dish out lots of freebies, so Holly, ever the sensible one, would have to remind him that they were trying to make money and run a business. It wouldn't have meant the end of his career. He could have worked from home; so many people did now, he could even have driven to the office a couple of times a week. Even though the last month they lived together had been unbearable he was clearly upset when she moved out. But he hadn't asked her to stay and appeared to accept her decision to leave.

Tess was still sitting dutifully at the door eyeing her new mistress testing out one of the mattresses. She'd been trained by the Baxters not to venture any further into the rooms.

Oops, Holly checked herself, *I've been sitting on the bed!* Quickly getting up, she brushed away the creases and fluffed up the pillows.

But as exciting as everything was, Holly couldn't ignore the well of loneliness seeping into her stomach. *I'm alone in this huge old house. There are so many rooms I haven't even decided which one will be mine. One thing's for sure. Tess will be sleeping with me tonight and every night. Supposing I find myself sleeping next door to an axe murderer?*

"C'mon Tess, let's go and get ourselves some supper."

As they rounded the stairs to the kitchen, she heard the phone ringing. Her stomach flipped as she hoped for a moment it would be Mac.

"Hey Hol, thought I'd come and see you. Jamie's going away on a training weekend with the Territorial Army next week. So, if you could use the company, I'll come down. Help you cook a few breakfasts and check out those guests."

"Oh, Janine that would be great. You can start with my American racing driver."

"American racing driver eh? Fab! I'll do a bit of research see what I can find out about him. What's his name?"

Holly spent the next few days in a tiz; cleaning and shampooing carpets, washing bed linen, airing bedrooms and making up beds. As much as she loved Tess and she certainly felt a lot safer for having her in the house, she was worried that the house could have a doggie smell. And doggie smells and guests did not mix.

***

Before she knew it, the day her American racing driver was expected, had arrived. Her fridge was filled with eggs, bacon, kippers, freshly squeezed orange juice, sausages, and hash browns. Holly had also stocked up on individual butter packs, jams and marmalades as well as bumper packs of croissants, in case he preferred a continental start to the day.

Around six pm the door-bell rang and Tess went berserk barking as Holly opened the door to her first guest. *Wow, he's gorgeous.* Tall and muscular, with a strong, handsome jawline, dark shaggy hair and perfect olive skin, Stuart Perone was dressed in blue jeans, a white T-shirt and navy blazer.

"Hi, I'm Stuart Perone," he said, offering her his hand. "I take it you are the proprietor, Holly Bradbury?" Their eyes locked for a moment and Holly thought she would keel over as the heat rushed to her embarrassed cheeks.

"Yes, that me," she managed to stammer as his firm masculine grip squeezed her small fingers. "Come in? Can I help you with your bags?"

"If you could take this small one, that would be great, thank you."

"Here we are," Holly said brightly, unlocking the door to her Wallflower Room. She gave him a quick tour of the room, pointing out the en suite bathroom, tea and coffee making facilities.

"Do you have a mini bar? Ice?" he asked expectantly.

Omg, Holly was momentarily floored.

"Actually, I don't." she stammered, explaining that this was a 'B&B' and she didn't have hotel facilities. He didn't look impressed.

"There is a pub opposite if you want to eat," she cut in quickly, "And I am sure I have some ice in my fridge." His deep, dark eyes bore into hers as they both knew he would have to pass on the ice because there wasn't a fridge in the room.

"What time would you like breakfast?" She asked brightly.

"Seven o'clock okay? I need to get to the track early. Get in a few laps before the race."

"Seven is fine," Holly answered. *God, I've got to get out of this room.* She felt completely overcome by his presence and she was sure he could sense her vulnerability around him.

"Is that one of your fine English pubs?" he asked, as he peered through the bedroom window at the Bulls Head opposite.

"Yes, it is," Holly answered adding that she was told it was very good. "You can get an evening meal there. Last orders for food is nine o'clock."

"You haven't eaten there yourself?"

"No, not yet. I have only just moved here." Holly was conscious she was starting to babble. *For goodness sake, she was acting more like a fifteen-year-old than a woman who had just hit thirty.* He was about to ask her something but his mobile phone rang and cut their conversation short.

"Hi Macey," he answered, "Yes I have arrived…" *Damn. It was a woman. Of course, a man like him would never be single.* Turning discreetly, she exited the room.

Chapter Four

Five thirty am the next morning, Holly was up and dressed ready to cook her first full English breakfast. She was up ridiculously early as Stuart Perone wasn't having breakfast until seven. Never mind, she busied herself polishing the cutlery and silver teapot and jug. Switching on the radio news she made herself a strong black coffee and pondered the day ahead. Tess had her breakfast and was in the garden. She didn't want her jumping up and barking madly when he came downstairs. The Women's Institute calendar the girls at work had bought her was on the kitchen wall and Holly circled the day's date, inscribing, '*Cooking first breakfast for first guest. A drop dead gorgeous American racing driver!*' Then she put on the 1950's style checked apron with the massive frills on the shoulders and hem. *What would Mac think if he saw me now? He'd be in the gym no doubt, working out before taking the tube to his plush offices.* She could picture him pounding away on the treadmill. Beads of sweat on his brow.

Shaking away all thoughts of him, she walked into the dining room to open the curtains. As the sun shone into the room it highlighted a rather pretty, shiny, silver snail trail which ran from under the table she'd laid for Stuart's breakfast across the carpet towards the room's huge, open fire place. *Dammit! I'll have to get rid of it quick before he comes down. How embarrassing if he catches me on my hands and knees wiping it up. Thank God for the kitchen paper; I'll grab that.* Just as she was frantically rubbing away the evidence she heard him coming down the stairs. As he opened the door into the dining room, there she was, scrubbing away, red faced and embarrassed.

"Good Morning, you must excuse me, I've just dropped one of my contact lenses."

As she stood up she trod on the frill of her W.I. pinny, the sound of ripping stiches adding to her flustered state as the frill hung down to just above her ankles.

"Oh, never mind, I'll sew it back later," she said brightly. Her cheeks crimson.

Stuart Perone's sensual mouth seemed to be suppressing a smile as Holly fought to preserve her dignity. His eyes drank her in as his gaze traced the elegant curves of her body beneath that ridiculous apron. It was the sort of thing his grandmother would wear.

"Now what can I get you? Tea? Coffee? A full English breakfast?"

"Just a couple of waffles and some maple syrup would do nicely," he answered, taking his seat, as directed, at the table by the window.

"Oh, er, I am so sorry," Holly stammered, "but I actually don't have any waffles or maple syrup. I can get you some for tomorrow?"

"Hey, no problem," he drawled in that sexy American accent. "Some strong black coffee and some of your English toast and marmalade will do nicely..."

"What about an egg? Can I at least get you an egg – poached, scrambled, boiled or sunny side up...?"

"Sunny side up?" he asked incredulously.

"Oh, that's just a silly English expression." Holly started to gabble. "When people have fried eggs and they ask for them to be 'sunny side up'... Oh, never mind..."

"No please carry on."

He clearly didn't want an egg and Holly was starting to feel very stupid. Especially as she couldn't really explain what the ridiculous saying meant.

"A lightly boiled egg will be fine," he said, holding her with his eyes.

"Right, a lightly boiled egg it is!" She said stepping back into the privacy of her kitchen.

Bloody thing! she cursed, ripping off the dangling frill and tossing it on a kitchen stool. *Oh god, I forgot to ask him if he wanted fruit juice. Oh, I'll just take a glass in with his egg.*

Sausages were sizzling in the pan in anticipation of an order for a full English breakfast. Plates were heating in the Aga; mushrooms, tomatoes, bacon and eggs were out ready to be cooked at the allotted time. *Dammit. Now I'll have to eat the sausages. Waffles indeed! This is England not America!*

Spying through the gap in the door, she could see he was looking at a few of the tourist leaflets he'd picked up from the hall. Thankfully, he seemed to be oblivious to the remnants of the snail trail glistening under his table.

Tearing away her gaze, she put a pan of water on to boil in preparation for his boiled egg. *God, I'm hopeless at boiling eggs. Mac liked his lightly boiled and complained that the ones she did for him were always rock hard. Was it three minutes or four? I can't give him an under-cooked one! Maybe I should give him two. That way one should be okay. Oh, why did I insist he had a bloody egg in the first place?* Trying to keep her cool, she cut the toast into neat triangles and popped them neatly into the toast rack. Her cheeks prettily flushed from her exertions in the kitchen, she stepped out into the dining room, tray in hand; politely placed his breakfast in front of him then raced back into the safety of her kitchen.

After about five minutes fretting at her kitchen sink, she plucked up enough courage to go back in and ask him if the wanted any more coffee and toast. But he'd gone and the eggs, which were clearly too hard for his taste, were half eaten.

"God how embarrassing!" Holly wailed on the phone to Janine later that morning. "His eggs were awful, he only ate half of them."
Janine could hardly speak for laughing.

"Oh dear, Hol, practice makes perfect! For God's sake don't burn his waffles tomorrow!"

"Let's hope he stays 'til tomorrow," Holly retorted, buttering herself a piece of toast and cutting up the cooked sausages for Tess as she cradled the phone to her ear.
"He doesn't seem to be too impressed so far!"

"Holly darling, tomorrow's breakfast will be perfect." Janine cooed encouragingly. "I did a little research on him. He's been racing professionally since he was seventeen and has made a lot of money through sponsorship – Gaff trainers and Jackson aftershave no less. He's out and about with the celebs in Manhattan. No mention of any girlfriend that I could see so, looks like he is single!"
A man like him would never be single. Holly wasn't deluding herself. Besides he wouldn't look twice at a country girl who as far as he knew, only knew how to cook eggs and bacon. Well, bacon...
But, Janine was right, his waffles were cooked to perfection the next morning.

Janine rang straight after her morning meeting at *'Smile'* magazine.

"So how did breakfast go this morning?"

"Breakfast was fine but he annoyed me." Holly said somewhat over-dramatically. He's been snooping around."

"Oh." Janine said flatly.

"Yes, I was just clearing away his breakfast plates

when he came rushing back into the dining room. Honestly, Janine, I thought he'd just witnessed a murder or something."

Everything was coming back to Holly in full techni-colour detail...

"That's a very fine car you have in your garage," he'd said.

"Yes' I know." Holly had smoothed her apron in defiance; she didn't like the tone of his voice.

"Would you be willing to sell?"

"I'd have to ask the owner." she replied as she stacked the dishwasher.

"So, it doesn't belong to you?"

"It's my father's."

He had followed her into the kitchen and was standing behind her as she stacked the plates in the dishwasher. His powerful presence was invading her space. Clearly, he thought she didn't know how much the car was worth. No doubt he thought he could swindle her.

"I'd give him a good price... a car like that should be driven regularly..."

"I'll pass your message on but I don't think he'll sell."

"He might for the right price?"

"You'd better get going or you are going to be late for your race." Holly remarked sweetly, indicating the kitchen clock.

Fixing her with a stare, he turned to go then stopped in the doorway.

"As I said, if he is willing to sell, I could offer an excellent price. Have a good day Miss Bradbury, and the waffles were excellent by the way."

The silver Bugatti Royale, Holly explained to a rapt Janine, belonged to Aunt Maud's brother, Will.

"It was his pride and joy. He used to hire it out to film companies and for weddings."
Considerably younger than his sister, she was devastated when he died from a heart attack at sixty years old, vowing that she would never sell her baby brother's prize possession. It remained in the garage of the house where she and Will had lived together for most of their adult lives.

"Mum said that however much she complained about lack of money, Aunt Maud was never tempted to sell her last links to Will. She left it to my Dad. But they don't have a garage so as soon as Aunt Maud's house was sold he drove it down here and parked it in my garage…I was worried he'd move in, just to guard it."

"Oh Holly," Janine laughed. "This is fab. Friction at Willow Cottage! And how does your racing driver like the quality of your bed sheets?"

"Ha ha. The only way he'll get his hands on that car is if he steals it and that wouldn't be a very good idea as its smothered with security lights and alarm systems. I also have his credit card and office details in New York… Hey ho, Life goes on… I'm fully booked next week," Holly said brightly, keen to change the subject. "Mrs Baxter continued taking bookings for me and there are some regulars who stay longer than one night, which is great because I don't have to keep changing the sheets!"

Chapter Five

"At last, I've come up with a headline," Janine gabbled on the phone as Holly was battling with her ironing later that afternoon. "Sleep shagging!"

"What?" asked Holly, distractedly, as she was trying to feed a sheet through the roller ball iron which Mrs Baxter had left for her because apparently it was brilliant for ironing sheets. The phone was balancing precariously under Holly's ear as she wrestled with the sheet. It was a delicate operation, especially with the rounded, rouched corners. Damn she just couldn't master this!

"Yes," continued Janine, "It's the one I told you about yesterday, randy husbands who don't know they are making love to their wives when they are asleep – you know, like a form of sleep-walking."

"Oh yes, I remember," said Holly, unwinding the sheet from the iron.

"Did you manage to find anyone who'd admit to such interesting activities?"

"Yes, little Marsha, from accounts. She talked her boyfriend into doing it. They can't pay their mortgage this month."

"My God!" Holly laughed, tossing the un-ironed sheet into the mounting ironing basket and throwing herself on the sofa.

The stories Margery wanted were becoming more and more bizarre, it was a hard job coming up with people like Marsha who would be associated with them in print. But the magazines were in hot competition, you had to keep them flying off the shelves. And if you wanted to keep your well-dressed little bottom on its designer seat, you had to come up with a never-ending supply of stories. This meant scouring through the newspapers for catchy news items that you could turn into some-thing bigger. Or, if you came across some-thing sensational, it was a race with the other magazines to get the story first; this meant luring the people in the story with handsome fees and the promise of five minutes fame.

But not all the stories were of the 'questionable' variety as Holly classified them; some were very sad, and when they appeared in print they often proved to be a lasting tribute to that lost loved one which could be very comforting for the people involved. Problems and issues were also high-lighted in the magazine, so it could be a great platform for a worthy cause. No two days were ever the same on 'Smile' magazine.

"Sleep Shagging," Holly mulled it over. "Yes, I can see that on the front cover... I saw a story in our local paper the other day about a pet rabbit which escapes into its neighbours' garden and terrorizes their cat. I could chase that one up for you. How about 'Thugs Bunny strikes again'..."

"Hey Hol, you haven't lost your touch, 'Thugs Bunny,' I like it. That could make a neat little filler... Just as Holly was getting carried away with the shenanigans of 'Thugs Bunny,' the doorbell rang.

"Oh my god!" squeaked Holly! Must be another guest!"

"How exciting!" said Janine.
Tess, barking loudly, was already at the door, jumping up and looking round for Holly as if to say, 'Where are you?' Holly quickly said good bye and went to answer the door; frantically smoothing her skirt and hair.

"Down Tess! down girl! Don't worry she's really a real gentle giant." Holly assured the pleasant middle-aged French couple standing in her door way. Luckily, they liked dogs.

"Good evening Madame, Iz it possible you 'as a room for ze night?"

"Er yes," Holly gabbled, "I've got..." her mind went blank... Which room would they like? "I er, have just moved in and..."

"So, you have a room for us?" His charming wife probed in her best English.

"Yes, I have several, sixteen in fact, er yes, follow me."

"What a beautiful house", the husband remarked, looking at all the pictures of English country scenes and antique tapestries adorning the walls left by the Baxters in the entrance hall. They were thrilled when Holly told them that the house had once been a sixteenth century coaching inn.

"Ah, so you must have Ghoulies then?" His wife asked, goggle-eyed. Holly twigged that she must have meant ghosts.

"Well, I'm not sure, I have only been here a few days but I haven't met any yet!" *Oh Lord, I don't want to frighten them off.* "Don't worry, the previous owners assured me there aren't any as the house is too busy." This seemed to assure the anxious looking wife who dutifully followed her husband, Holly and Tess up the winding stairs to view her rooms. The husband thought it was highly amusing that Holly had just moved in.

"So, we are her first guests!" He said, laughing to his wife. (Holly didn't want to correct him by saying they were really her second).

"We'd better behave ourselves then!"
His wife didn't understand his English so he translated in French for his wife's benefit.

"Oh, la la, so we are your first guests!" his wife repeated, laughing. Holly saw the funny side and laughed too.

Holly offered them a choice of rooms.

"This is the 'Delphinium'... the 'Marguerite'... and this is the 'Passion Flower' Room."

"The 'Passion Flower' room eh?" The husband laughed, "Maybe tonight will be my lucky night!"

"Er yes," Holly agreed, somewhat embarrassed.

"They are all very beautiful Madame. This one will be fine." said the husband genially, bouncing his bottom on the bed. It was quite a hike going up all those stairs with their cases and they didn't want to climb any more to the next floor. Holly showed them how to work the shower and television and pointed out the tea and coffee making facilities. She then gave them two keys; one for their room and one for the front door which she said she always kept locked, so she would be grateful if they locked it when they went in and out of the house.

Tess sat dutifully at the door to the room.

"What time is breakfast?" The husband asked.

Holly hadn't thought about this. "What time would you like it?"

"Eight o'clock?" the wife suggested.

"Eight o'clock it is then," said Holly brightly. "Full English or Continental?"

"Full English of course." they laughed.

"Great! The dining room is the first room on the right as you come in the front door. See you tomorrow, have a lovely day."

"I've done it Tess, welcomed my first guests," Holly said gleefully as she danced down the winding stairs. (It had all been a bit different with Stuart Perone as he had been booked in).

Checking her watch, Holly saw that it had just turned four o'clock. She was running short of kitchen paper. If she hurried up she could make it to the 'Cash 'n' Carry' for a quick shop. But it was a beautiful afternoon and Tess was looking at her expectantly.

"Come on," she said, grabbing Tess's lead from the coat-stand near the ironing room. "Let's go and get some country air."

How beautiful it was walking over the fields. Cows were grazing so she couldn't let Tess off her lead. The cleanest, clearest water babbled in tiny brooks and streams and bunches of wild watercress were growing in the shallowest parts of the water. Walking further on through the fields, she came to Fishbourne Creek. It was from here, Holly realised, that the pirates would set off in their boats with their booty – she could just picture them tying up their boats under the cover of darkness then running through the fields to the secret tunnel to Willow Cottage delivering their wares to the Brewery.

Rounding the corner past Fishbourne's quaint, twelfth century church, Holly noticed a couple of wild, brown rabbits happily hopping in the sun. Even though Tess was such a huge dog Mrs Baxter said she didn't need much walking and was happy with a twenty-minute trek over the fields. She'd then plop happily back in her basket with a dog chew and spend the rest of the day in and out of the back garden.

"Well, you've had a good walk today old girl, we've been out at least an hour."

"Afternoon Tess," said a pleasant looking middle-aged lady who was walking a beautiful Alsatian; "Hello, You must be the new owner of Willow cottage?"

"Yes, I am. Holly Bradbury. How do you do?" Holly shook her hand.

"I'm Vera Croft, from Fishbourne Post Office, glad to say we're not shut down yet!"

"You're not expecting to be, are you?" Holly asked, not a little surprised. So many village post offices were closing down all over the country.

"Well, the arrival of Tesco isn't good for us, but there are a lot of elderly people in Fishbourne who don't have transport to get into Chichester, so hopefully we'll survive."

"I do hope so," said Holly genuinely, as the two women chatted about the village post office being the hub of village life.

Vera's dog, Lady, was gorgeous, a great shaggy Alsatian.

"We're so pleased you have kept Tess. Lady would have missed her dreadfully."

The dogs were indeed very friendly, dancing in mad circles around each other before bounding into the water together after imaginary sticks. As they walked on, three other dog owners introduced themselves and their canine companions. All said how happy they were that Tess was still resident at Willow Cottage.

There was Nick, who ran 'The Woolpack Inn' with his chocolate-brown Labrador, Murphy, who the regulars loved in the pub.

"Have you tried our famous 'O'Hagan' sausages?" He asked Holly. "They're the best in West Sussex. Might go down well with your guests as they are all locally sourced. I'll drop a pack in to you."

"That would be lovely, thank you."

"Ah, there's our wonderful Miss Brannan, she teaches my grandchildren at Fishbourne Primary. Always walks little Bella after school."

"My goodness, teachers were never that glamorous when I was at school." Holly remarked.

"Yes, and she has a very good-looking mum and grandma. All the kids love her. I think my grand-daughter, Jessica has a bit of a crush on her."

Holly could see why. She was delightful, apologising profusely for her cute little bundle of fluff annoying Lady and Tess.

"Leave them alone Bella, they don't want to play. I'm so sorry, Bella, come here."

"Stop being so mean, you were a puppy once," Vera chided Lady.

"How do you do, I'm Emily," Miss Brannan said, shaking hands with Holly.

"How do you do. Lovely to meet you. I'm Holly. What breed is Bella?"

"She's a Lhasa Apso. Very friendly, I took her into class the other day for one of our 'Show and Tell' sessions. The kids loved her." We have a teddy bear they take home to write about but now they all want to take Bella home instead! Caused a few problems with the mums and dads I'm afraid…"

"So, anyway," Vera, cut in, "Have you met your resident ghost yet?"
Emily immediately gave Vera a disapproving look as Holly's heart missed a beat.

"Ghost? Oh god, no!"

"Nothing to worry about," Emily added quickly, sensing Holly's distress. Susan used to joke about her all the time. Said she was harmless."
Vera agreed enthusiastically, completely unaware that Holly was quaking in her flip flops.

"She reckons its Miss Gibbons, the old Victorian school 'marm'. Nothing bad happens, she's just seen her walking up the outside stairs to the old school room. 'Said she hovers about in there sometimes."

"Must have been really dedicated to the job." Emily joked.

"Oh no, that's where I'm going to have my sewing room."

"Play some loud music in there. They don't like music, by all accounts." Emily added, trying to make Holly feel better.

"Good idea. She'll soon shove off though, once you have a house full of guests. Come along now Lady, we'd better get back. See you soon, girls." Vera bounced off, singing to herself with Lady at her side.

"Oh no, are you worried now?" Emily asked kindly.

"A bit," Holly admitted.

"Maybe speak to the vicar? See if he can come and bless the room? They do that sometimes. Sounds like poor Miss Gibbons needs a bit of help getting out of that school room."

"Good idea."

"Don't worry too much, Vera does exaggerate, lovely to meet you Holly, I'm sure we'll bump into each other again." And with that she sauntered off. A golden angel gliding through the fields with her lovely little Bella.

A bloody ghost, that's all I need. Holly reflected as she threw a stone into the water for Tess to fetch. *I can handle awkward guests but I'm not sure about a ghost…*

"Typical. Just my luck eh Tess?"

Tess was looking at her expectantly, with the stone in her mouth. As Holly threw it in the shimmering water and watched her bound in after it she realised that she was now a confirmed dog lover and hadn't regretted taking on Tess for a moment. It was so easy to meet people if you had a dog and not only was she a wonderful companion, she made Holly feel safer. If she didn't hear the doorbell, Tess would find her, wherever she was in the house. No uninvited guests would dare come in with Tess about. Not that she would hurt anybody; she was indeed the 'gentlest giant,' but Holly wasn't going to tell everyone that.

Filling her lungs with the cool sweet air, Holly's thoughts turned to Stuart Perone. *He'd be racing round the tracks now. If he comes back in a bad mood I'll know he lost. Why is it so many attractive men can be such a pain? And the cheek of it – him snooping in my garage and asking all those questions.*

You can do it. You have to do it. Holly took a deep breath and opened the door gingerly into Miss Gibbons' old school room.

"Come on Tess, come in." Tess waddled in, not in the least bit perturbed. So far so good. Holly was going to spend the evening sorting through the room. It was full up with paint pots and ladders left by the Baxters. *So nice of them to leave this for me.* The picture of Miss Gibbons and her school children was still clinging on the wall. Taking it down and dusting it thoughtfully, Christine Baxter's words resonated in her ears; *'Buried in the churchyard she is...Probably along with some of them little nippers...'*

What became of you? Holly asked the little blonde girl, standing to attention at the edge of the group. She could only have been about five. *And what about you?* Holly wondered aloud as she studied the face of a young boy who looked like he had stepped straight out of a Dickens' novel. *Had they spent their lives here in Fishbourne or moved away? Had they been happy? Were any of them destined to be childhood sweethearts?* When Holly had painted the room, she'd hang the picture above her beloved Singer sewing machine.

"I'm sure we can tolerate each other Miss Gibbons. This will always be your school room. I'm just going to tidy up a bit and put my sewing stuff in here. Did you teach sewing? I bet you did. You know, I think I'm going to get one of those little school desks with ink wells. I'll put it in here for you, and maybe a blackboard? I think you'd like that."

The room suddenly felt very cold and Holly had a strong sense that someone was standing behind her.

Tess barked. But when Holly turned around no one was there.

Right, time for some music! Holly put 'Ed Sheeran' on very loudly and sang along to *'Thinking out Loud.'* Forcing thoughts of Miss Gibbons out of her mind, she cleaned the grimy walls with sugar soap in preparation for their being painted a pale buttery yellow. Holly was on a roll. Absorbed in her cleaning and oblivious to time, she stopped for a cup of tea couple of hours later. Peeking out the window she couldn't see any sign of Stuart's car. Not that she'd see it anyway as it was really dark now.

She'd just gone down stairs and was heading for the kitchen when Stuart's key rattled in the door.

"You're up late Miss Bradbury, still working I see... Stand still a moment," he said, moving closer to her...

"What? What is it?"

"Don't panic, just stand still..."

Holly was panicking. He was standing right in front of her staring intently at the top of her head. A minute later he picked a huge spider from out of her hair. Cupping it gently in his hand he put it outside the front door where it scuttled out into the garden.

"Omg! Thank you." Holly's knees felt weak. She had a horror of spiders.

"No problem, he said ascending the stairs to his room. "Have a goodnight's sleep and no dreaming of spiders." He smiled.

Chapter Six

Despite the incident with the spider, Holly fell asleep as soon as her head hit the pillow and had no recollection of any nasty dreams when she woke up the next morning. However, Stuart standing so close to her, tenderly picking that horrible spider out of her hair, there was no forgetting that.
A quick shower helped clear her head. Pulling on jeans and a crisp white shirt, she applied a quick dab of translucent face powder, some lipstick and mascara. Never did she think the day would come when she would face the world without foundation, but her 'city skin' had turned a nice golden brown after her daily walks in the fields with Tess.

Everything was progressing nicely, there were no snail trails in sight and Holly's French couple were munching their cereal happily in the dining room, discussing their plans for the day while Holly started cooking their sausages and bacon. But then she burnt their toast and set the fire alarm off. The noise was deafening and while she was frantically waving at the smoke alarm to dispel the smoke, she burnt their bacon as well.

"Olly? Olly? Is everything okay?" Mr Frenchman asked, poking his head around the kitchen door.

"Yes, yes, fine. I just burnt some toast and that set the fire alarm off," Holly answered, still frantically waving a tea towel at the smoke alarm. Mrs Frenchman then appeared with a hanky over her nose because of the smoke. Luckily, they saw the funny side.
Mrs Frenchman nearly wet herself laughing while they were babbling in French.
Holly meanwhile, had rushed out to the hall to re-set the fire alarm only to be met by Stuart coming down

the stairs to breakfast.

"Hi there. Is everything alright?"

"Good morning," *Oh lord, that sounded so formal, so English...* "Oh yes, fine, don't worry, I just burnt some toast and set off the smoke alarm. These things are very sensitive."

"Have you managed to re-set it?" He asked, spotting the instruction manual in her hands.

"Yes, I have. Thank you. Everything is okay now," Holly answered, acutely aware that her cheeks had turned scarlet. Tess was barking frantically to be let in from the back garden and Holly felt like screaming.

"Are you all set for your race?"

"Sure," Stuart replied, "Just going to check on your British weather."

Slipping into his seat he checked the weather conditions on his tablet as Holly disappeared into the kitchen to get his coffee and waffles. Just as she put everything on his table a large drop of water splashed from the ceiling onto his tablet. Holly froze as he ostentatiously flicked the drop away.

"I am so sorry." she gushed.

"Looks like you've got a leak, better be careful your ceiling doesn't crash down on your guests Miss Bradbury."

He ate his waffles in silence, then picked up his tablet, thanked her curtly for his breakfast and exited the dining room. Moments later, Holly heard him driving down her drive.

Mr and Mrs Frenchman silently finished their coffee, pretending to be oblivious to everything while Holly cooked them another breakfast.

As soon as she'd served them she raced up to Stuart's room, which was directly above the dining room.

Her heart sank as she looked at the sodden carpet.

Oh Lord, should I move his things out into another room

or wait until he's back? He might be really annoyed if I touch anything.

Just as she was coming out of his room, the French couple were coming up the stairs.

Not being able to help herself, Holly burst into tears.

"Oh la, la 'Olly, what iz de matter?" Mrs Frenchman rushed over and put her arm around her.

"There's a leak in the shower in one of my guest's rooms and its dripping into the dining room," Holly wailed.

Mr Frenchman, following his wife's orders, purposefully marched into Stuart's room, closely followed by Mrs Frenchman, who was waving him in. Mrs Frenchman took great delight at casting her eye over Stuart's possessions. Crisp cotton shirts, cashmere sweaters, designer T-shirts and jeans were all neatly hung on hangers in the wardrobe. *Oh lord, please don't touch any of his stuff, it would be just my luck if he comes back now.*

Mr Frenchman was in the shower surveying the shower head and tapping the wall while Mrs Frenchman was 'oohing' and 'ahhing' at the quality of Stuart's clothes. *I can't deal with this, I should just call a plumber...*

Mr Frenchman was gesticulating dramatically until Holly realised he was after a spanner and screwdriver. Running down the stairs she grabbed her tool box from the ironing room. Giving her the thumbs up Mr Frenchman neatly removed a couple of tiles on the shower wall, while Holly, was on tenterhooks, still fretting that Stuart would come back and catch them all in his room.

After what seemed an eternity, Mr Frenchman found the leaking pipe, tightened the nut and after a bit of tidying up, came out of the shower cubicle looking triumphant. He'd stopped the leak. *Oh, thank God.* Holly gave him a big hug. Now the wife was taking out hangers of clothes from Stuart's wardrobe and gesticulating towards other rooms. *Yes, maybe, she's right, we should move his things out now, he won't want to be doing this late at night...*

Holly pointed to the room and she and Mrs Frenchman sprang into action moving Stuart's things in there while Mr Frenchman came out of Stuart's old room with the tool box.

It was just at that moment that they heard footsteps coming up the stairs.

"Stuart," Holly stammered, her face turning scarlet.

"Where are you going with my clothes?"

"I am so sorry, your shower is leaking, the carpet is wet and I didn't know what time you'd get back so..."

"You know Miss Bradbury, if you want to run a successful business your reputation is everything. You have to provide people with showers that work and ceilings that don't leak all over their breakfast."

"Now give me my clothes," he said defiantly.

"Where to now?"

Holly showed him into the Gardenia Room.

"But this isn't en suite."

"Err no, but there is a bathroom and toilet that no one else is using just down the hall there."

He wasn't impressed.

"I can move the rest of my things myself, thank you."

Luckily Monsieur and Madame Duvalle weren't in a hurry to leave. They were such a lovely couple and tried to get Holly to see the funnier side of things that morning, insisting that she sat down in the dining room and had some coffee with them. They told her they had a daughter around her own age who worked in marketing in Paris and were surprised and impressed at Holly's decision to turn her hand to something so different from her previous career.

"You 'ave no have husband 'Olly? You live 'ere alone?" Madame Duvalle had asked, incredulously. Holly blushed.

"Well yes, I may not have a husband but I do have a dog."

"Oh, la la," said Madame Duvalle, and delving into her handbag she pulled out a picture of a jovial looking, if a little portly, French farmer with a very red face.

"You must come over to France 'Olly and meet our son Bertram. He needs a good wife."

Helping them with their cases to their car and promising she would give them a call when she was next in Paris, Holly waved the Duvalles on their way. She felt quite bereft at their parting. It was good having people like them in the house.

After all the drama of the morning, Holly had forgotten to let Tess in.

"Oh Tess," she said, breaking Mrs Baxter's very strict rule and letting her into the dining room as they made their way back into the house. "I mucked up this morning! Here girl, have this," she said, popping a triangle of toast left by the French couple into the dog's mouth. "Who'd have thought cooking a few breakfasts could be so stressful?"

If I had any brandy I'd have one.

Baulking at the memory of her encounter with Stuart that morning, she sipped her coffee in contemplative silence. He was right. A good reputation was everything in this game.

Stuart could ruin her business with a bad review. *He's probably posted something already. This is my third day as a B&B Queen, and so far, I've notched up a trauma every day!*

Checking her watch, Holly saw that it was getting on for lunch time and Madge, the cleaning lady she had inherited from the Baxters was coming in at two pm. There was just time for a quick sandwich and escape to the fields with Tess. If ever Holly needed some reviving country air it was today.

It was a lovely walk, she felt a lot calmer and even managed to see the funny side after her eventful morning. There was obviously a lot more to running a B&B than Holly ever imagined. They were just passing the duck pond on their way back to the house when she saw a jovial looking lady huffing and puffing her way towards them.

"I'm Madge," she said extending her plump little hand.

"Oh Madge, pleased to meet you! I'm Holly."
Tess, obviously knew Madge well, and bounded up to her as they made their way up the garden path to the house.

"Okay Tess, down darling, I've got your bissie!" Madge said fondly, unwrapping a dog biscuit from her pocket as they stepped into the house. "Ooh it's a bootiful morning," she said, making her way into the little ironing-room where she hung up her jacket, put on her pinny and changed her shoes.

"So how are you settling in?"

"Oh, very well thank you," enthused Holly, as she started to tell her all about Stuart, the French people, burning the toast and the alarm going off.

"You'll get used to everything," Madge said genially as she collected her little box with cleaning fluids, dusters, polish and strangely, a perming comb.

An additional bag contained tea bags, sachets of coffee and mini milks plus a packet of paper doilies to place at the bottom of each room's waste-paper basket.

"Which rooms are there today then dear?" She looked and sounded like 'Miss Piggy' from The Muppets, with her squeaky little voice, plump cheeks and snub nose.

"Just the 'Gardenia' to tidy and the 'Passion Flower' Room to change today. But we've got the 'Delphinium' and 'The Marguerite' room booked for tonight so if you could check they are okay that would be great. Mrs Baxter very kindly made up all the rooms but they might need a quick airing. Oh, and if you could hoover the landings and check the stairs please Madge."

"Righto, could you be a love and bring the hoover up for me?"

To her dismay, Holly realised that because of her size, Madge couldn't carry the hoover. So, while Madge huffed and puffed her way up the stairs with the cleaning box and bag of extras Holly had to carry the hoover.

"If you could just help me with the sheets love? Mrs Baxter always gave me the sheets, it's so difficult to know which are the right size." Madge apologised.

"Of course," said Holly opening the linen cupboard. Pillow-cases, sheets and duvets were neatly ironed and folded in stacks but Holly had no idea which were doubles or singles. There were no labels saying what was what. She'd have to unfold them and see. Until she got her bumper delivery of crisp, white Egyptian cotton sheets, the Passion Flower room, would have to have coral-coloured bedlinen and peach towels. When they went to make up the bed Holly found that the duvet cover was a double but the sheet was a single. Dammit she'd have to refold it and hope it didn't look used. *What a pain if I have to iron it again.*

Once they'd got the sheets in order Holly had to help Madge make the beds up because she was just too big to reach over it. This is ridiculous I shouldn't be spending my time helping a hired help. She could have been off to the Cash'n'Carry by now, stocking up on eggs and bacon and hash-browns. If Mac had been here he would have given Madge 'her cards' as he put it, straight away.

Before Holly knew it, it was four o'clock and she thought she'd better invite Madge down for a cup of tea. A very pink-faced 'Miss Piggy' descended in the dining room, a little tub of saccharin tablets in her pudgy hand. But she was so sweet, Holly couldn't help taking to her. As they chatted over coffee she told Holly she was a widow and now lived with her aged mother who was very demanding, and her work at Willow Cottage was a welcome break. Madge, like Tess, was indeed part of the fixtures and fittings that came with Willow Cottage, Holly thought kindly as she dipped her ginger biscuit into her coffee. Thinking of 'fixtures and fittings' Holly realised she had been short-changed by the Baxter's. She was short of at least two televisions, a couple of bedside tables, a lamp and kettle.

"He was a nasty piece of work," Madge remarked, referring to Mr Baxter, as she popped her saccharin pills in her coffee.

"Gave Bob a right 'ard time."
Bob, she explained, was the Baxter's lodger. He had been living at Willow Cottage for seven years and had the small room under the stairs that Holly had turned into her ironing room.

"He said he wouldn't move out when they sold the house, so Mr Baxter got his cronies round and beat poor young Bob black and blue. Smashed up his room they did. He went to the police and they escorted him back to the house, but the Baxter's made his life hell, so in the end he went".

Holly was horrified. When she first made an offer on the property, her solicitor said she shouldn't go ahead because it wouldn't be a vacant possession. Two weeks later they heard the property was vacant and so the deal went ahead. Looking back Holly remembered how Mrs Baxter didn't show her what must have been Bob's room.

'Oh, you don't want to be bothered looking in there,' she'd said, 'It's just a tiny box room full of junk.'

"Mrs Baxter did all the work." Madge continued, "Never saw him up before midday. Then he'd be off 'doing the horses.' Most he'd ever do was walk Tess and go to the Cash'n'Carry. Never saw him clean any rooms or cooking any breakfasts, even when she was pregnant and had the baby, but he was a devil for checking the rugs – all them fringes had to be combed straight. That's why they got them perming combs. Nothing like 'em for combing fringes on rugs straight. Go mad, he would if they weren't combed straight. Anyway, as I was sayin'... Think there was trouble with money too." Madge said, conspiratorially, adding: "They had to get out quick."

"That figures," said Holly, "I've had a few calls already from people asking where they are. A bailiff knocked on the door the other day too. Poor Mrs Baxter, Holly reflected, her man in the country didn't turn out to be such a good catch.

'Whatever you do, don't get behind on the washing,' Christine Baxter's words resounded in Holly's ears as Holly sipped her coffee the next morning. Happily, breakfast had passed without any incidents. Stuart pointedly picked a table away from any possible re-occurrence of a leak in the ceiling. But he was quite complimentary about his breakfast and even joked

about Holly having any more encounters with spiders. So, she concluded that he must have forgiven her. *The bloody washing, that is definitely the worst part of being a B&B Queen*, Holly reflected as she watched a little robin hop on the bird table through the dining room window. *Oh Lord… and the windows need cleaning. How the heck am I going to clean a hundred odd windows?*

But the sun was shining, so she decided she'd load up the washing machine so the sheets and towels could dry outside. Janine was due to call for her morning update on the goings on at Willow Cottage and Holly wanted the washing on before she called. *Oh well, at least my little mishaps make Janine laugh.*
But her friend didn't sound her usual bubbly self that morning.

"Margery's retiring in three months, Oh, Hol, I wish you'd stayed. You'd have been editor, it would have been so great…"

"Well, I may have to sack myself, so tell Margery I'll be after her job," Holly laughed, good naturedly. "So, come on, why are you so worried?"

"S'posing the new editor makes a clean sweep? You know how it is, brings in a load of new people and gets rid of a load of us."
Holly did her best to reassure her that things would be fine. Under Holly's mentoring Janine had proved herself a valuable member of the team. She'd got through her probation period with flying colours and was now permanently employed as a staff writer on the magazine.

"So anyway, how were your guests today? Any more dramas with the racing driver?"
Holly took a deep breath. She didn't know where to start…

***

Holly was just traipsing down the garden to her washing line with a bundle of bed linen after nattering to Janine when Stuart drove back up the drive, the gentle breeze blowing back his shiny dark hair.

"Just popped back to get my Saint Christopher," he called out his car window, "Never race without it." Holly smiled, conscious that her top had ridden up a little as she stretched to peg the heavy sheets on the line.

"Here, let me give you a hand," he said gallantly, shaking a scrunched-up duvet cover from the washing basket which he threw effortlessly over the line and pegged perfectly. "There you go." he said, hanging up the last pillow case. "This must keep you fit," he said, his eyes scanning her breasts and delicious curve of her well-toned stomach. "Quite hard work, isn't it?"

"Had any more thoughts about the car?" he called back cheekily as he walked to his car.

As Holly stood trance-like, watching this infuriating man pull down the soft top on his Mercedes before driving back to the race track, Madge, carrying her cleaning box, called Holly back to reality.

"You alright luv? Someone hasn't done a runner, have they?"

"Oh no, no." Holly assured her, I was just saying good bye to our racing driver…"

"Oh yes, he be a good looker ain't he." Madge gushed, trying to gauge Holly's reaction.

"You can't help notice a good-looking chap like that, not many about like him…"

"Yes, well, I think we'd better see what's happened to our absent guest." Holly cut in, feeling horribly prim.

Mr Wainwright, a travelling greetings card sales-man who had regular clients in Chichester and was a long-time regular guest of the Baxter's, had checked in late last night and was supposed to come down for a late breakfast at nine. It was past midday and there was no sign of him. Madge had to tidy his room before they had coffee or they would never get the rooms ready for the wedding party Holly was expecting at the weekend.

"Think we should knock on the door luv, time's ticking on," Madge remarked.

Holly thought for a moment, she didn't want to be too intrusive. Maybe he'd decided to skip breakfast. If it got to one o'clock and he still hadn't come down, she'd knock on his door. In the meantime, Holly would do some ironing and Madge could hoover the stairs and landing.

When it got to one o'clock, Holly trudged up the stairs preparing for action. *After all, I'm running a business and guests should vacate hotel rooms by midday...* She had just rounded the stairs when, to her horror, she saw Madge peeking through the key hole into his room. *OMG, supposing he suddenly opened the door?* Madge would be flung down the stairs, her butter-ball little body, landing in an unconscious heap of wobbling pink blancmange in the hall.

"His big toe's poking out of the sheet, it's stayed in the same position since the last time I looked," she squeaked.

"How long ago was that?"

"About fifteen minutes..."

Holly dropped down on her haunches and looked through the key hole. There it was; standing tall and rigid just like Madge said. There were no other signs of movement in the room.

"Oh God, Madge, what should we do?" Holly could see the scene now. Undertakers in dark suits turning up with a body bags to remove poor old Mr Wainwright in the early hours. Then, no doubt he'd come back to haunt her and Tess, who would literally, go barking mad and never be the same again.

"Supposing he is dead? What about his wife? I'll have to tell her."

Holly felt the colour drain from her cheeks while Madge busied herself dusting nowhere in particular.

"Right, that's it, I'll have to get the key and go in." Holly said, resolutely, bending down to take another peek. Then, bam! a large bulk was walking towards the door which suddenly opened.

"Oh, Good morning!" Holly jumped up awkwardly, suppressing a shriek. Madge screamed, clutching her feather duster to her ample bosom.

Dressed in his dressing gown Mr Wainwright surveyed them sleepily, his hair all ruffled.

"I'm so sorry Ladies, I overslept, is it too late for breakfast?"

Holly was so relieved, she said that was fine. *Thank, God he is alive.* Madge was rooted to the spot. Her face was bright red, she was breathing rapidly and dramatically fanning her face. As Mr Wainwright, oblivious to everything, made his way into the bathroom next door, the two women hastily made their way back to the kitchen, desperately trying to compose themselves.

"Thank god I don't have to get in the undertakers." Holly giggled, making them both a coffee while poaching two eggs for Mr Wainwright.

"Mrs Baxter would never cook breakfast this late Holly," Madge chided her fondly.

He certainly wasn't in any hurry to get to work. By the time Holly and Madge had tidied his room, neatly rearranging his 'Givenchy Gentleman' toiletries, making his bed, emptying his bin, washing the sink, straightening the towels and replenishing the tea, coffee and milk sachets, he was still lingering over his breakfast.

The sun was shining and Tess was looking at Holly expectantly.

"Oh, come on old girl," Holly said, clipping her lead to her collar. "Let's go and get our daily dose of country air. It's going to be a busy weekend with our wedding party, we may not get much of a walk tomorrow."

By the time they got back from their walk, Madge had gone but Holly wanted to check that the rooms were up to scratch for her guests later that day. And she was very glad she did because the towels didn't match in Stuart's room. Madge had only put out one sachet of coffee instead of two. She hadn't polished the mirror in the shower – it still had splash marks on it and horror of all horrors, the en suite shower in the 'Honeymoon suite,' had hair in the plug.

She didn't want to turn into an old bag complaining that one just '*Couldn't get the right staff nowadays*,' so she'd decided that from now on she'd just have to check the rooms every day after Madge went home. She could just hear Mac taking her to task for being so soft and then talk of the devil the phone rang.

"Willow Cottage," she answered brightly.

"Good Afternoon Willow Cottage," Mac answered. "I'll have my eggs sunny side up, please."

"Oh, Hi Mac," Holly couldn't deny that she was pleased to hear from him.

"God Hol, it's been such a stressful week. "We've got to pitch against two other agencies to keep our 'Splash' rainwear account. If we lose this one there will be redundancies."

There was a strained pause in the conversation.

"I've missed you Hol, thought I'd drive down tonight, we could go out for dinner, walk along the beach, just the two of us...?"
Against her better judgement, Holly agreed. It was going to be a busy weekend but she was starting to tire of her own company, and with a boisterous wedding party, it would feel good to have Mac about. She drove into Chichester and bought some white wine, mussels and spaghetti. She wanted Mac to fall in love with the magic of the house and would talk him out of going out to eat.

**

The wedding party arrived later that day. The bride was staying at her family home in Bosham, while the groom, his parents and best man were staying at Willow Cottage. They were all utterly delightful. The groom, who looked around twenty-five, was a dentist. His best man, a vet, immediately took to Tess, remarking that not many people had Bullmastiffs nowadays. He and Holly talked at length about the breed, their likes and dislikes and how much exercise they should have. After he had disappeared upstairs with their cases, the groom's parents remarked proudly to Holly that their future daughter-in-law was 'a gorgeous young woman' and they couldn't be more thrilled that she was to be their daughter-in-law.
How lovely, Holly thought wistfully, yet not without a little touch of the old green-eyed monster. *Some girls just get things right. A perfect husband and charming in-laws. How wonderful to be on the cusp of such wonderful memories, yet to be made.*

The wedding was going to take place in the tiny Norman Church of Saint Peter's, across the fields from Willow Cottage, followed by the reception in the beautiful, Millstream Hotel. The happy couple would spend the night there before flying off to Honeymoon in Sri Lanka, but the best man and the groom's parents would be returning to Willow Cottage to stay an extra night before driving back to Yorkshire.

Time was ticking on and Holly was just about to start scrubbing the beards off the mussels in preparation for her dinner with Mac when the phone rang.

"Sorry babe, I can't come down tonight. I've got to put a lot more work into this bloody pitch. It's going to have to be tomorrow now..."

Holly felt as though a brick had been dropped in her stomach. She'd made such an effort. It was Friday night and she was alone, everyone she knew was out partying or cosying up to their boyfriends. *What had happened to Holly Bradbury? The highlight of her week-end would be walking Tess, battling with sheets and cooking bloody eggs and bacon. No doubt he wouldn't make it tomorrow either.* She was annoyed she was so upset and didn't know whether to believe him or not.

The conversation didn't end happily and Holly chucked the mussels in the bin. Putting her arms round Tess, Holly sobbed into her huge neck. You could always rely on your dog to love you.

"Oh darling," Janine soothed her troubled friend, on the phone, a few minutes later. "Look, how about I come down and keep you company tonight? Jim is away on one of his bloody Territorial Army weekends again."

"Oh, would you? I'd love to see you! I've got a wedding party this weekend, there're all so bloody happy I could do with a friend!"

"Great, I'll see you in a couple of hours. I'll bring us some treats."

True to her word, a couple of hours later, Janine tottered to the door in her high heels clutching a large bottle of wine and massive box of chocolates.

"Wow Hol, this is amazing," she said kissing her long-lost buddy on both cheeks. "I had no idea it was so huge!! Oh my god, who's this?" she asked in mock fright when she saw Tess.

Holly assured her she was a lot more docile then she looked then led her into her sitting room, showing her the dining room, kitchen and ironing room on the way.

"God, no wonder you are always ironing," Janine exclaimed as she saw the neatly piled tower of sheets.

"Yeah, that's the worst part of running a B&B, but it's okay if you listen to the radio," Holly said, popping open the cork and hugging Janine once more, even though they spoke most days on the phone, she didn't realise how much she'd missed her.

They had a wonderful evening, tucking into a large mound of spaghetti and meatballs topped off, by the top layer of the box of chocolates Janine brought.

"So, how's Jim?"

Janine wrinkled her pert little nose and thought for a moment.

"He's married to the bloody Territorial Army, I hardly ever see him ... to tell you the truth, Hol, I'm still not over my first love."

"Oh Janine, I'm so sorry, what happened?"

Janine took a deep breath.

"I met Mark at university. It was love at first sight. For me, anyway," she smiled. "We spent all our time with each other outside lectures and talked about a future together." Her voice faltered but she continued. "After we graduated we both got jobs. Me, on a local paper, Mark, on a well-known business to business magazine. It wasn't long before he was headhunted and offered a job on a sister magazine in the States. He wanted me to go with him but my mum had just been diagnosed with cancer. I couldn't go Hol, the timing just wasn't right... He said he understood and would wait for me to say when the time was right but four months later he moved in with a girl he met there."

"That must have been awful."

"Yes, it was. I still torture myself thinking about it. You know, with the old 'what ifs?'"

"Yes, I know all about the 'what ifs?"

"I had to change things quickly, get away from all the memories. It saved my life when you offered me my job. Trouble is, I still think about him and no one else seems to match up to Mark...Jim and I have been together for six months," Janine sighed. "Things aren't so hot outside the bedsheets Hol. He isn't interested in my world and frankly, I have to push myself to be interested in his."

Shades of Mac and me. Holly reflected sadly.

"Mr Right will come along, probably when you least expect it. You are far too gorgeous to be single for long."

"You too, my friend," Janine added softly.

Talk then turned to the magazine and Margery's impending retirement.

"You could still be the new editor?" Janine asked hopefully.

Holly explained that she'd reached a point in her life when she wanted things to change. After her miscarriage, she viewed her life differently; her heart was no longer in to the shenanigans of '*Smile*' magazine.

"But don't you get lonely Hol, down here all on your own?" Janine asked, tucking her long legs up on the sofa, *God, it was so good to get out of those shoes.*

"Yes, I do but I've got Tess and life is never dull, what with thinking one of your guests has died on you and never knowing who is going to turn up at your door."

"Well, at least you've got the diversion of a handsome guest!" Janine laughed as she pinched the last chocolate.

"True." Holly had to agree.

It was nearly one in the morning by the time the two girls headed for bed, trying not to laugh and giggle too much going up the stairs in case they woke up the guests.

Chapter Seven

Janine was an absolute darling the next morning and insisted on helping Holly with the breakfasts. So, while Holly cooked the bacon and eggs Janine got stuck-in making toast, coffee and tea.

"Phwor, he's a bit of all right?" she remarked, coming back in to the kitchen after giving the wedding party their tray of tea.

"You can keep your hands off the groom," Holly laughed, biting into a spare sausage and giving Janine a cup of tea.

"Please tell me it's not him!" Janine whispered, pointing through the crack in the door to the dining room.

Holly, looked through to check.

"No, He's the best man. Um, yes, he is rather nice," Holly agreed, watching him bite into his toast. "Wonder if he's single? He hasn't come down with anyone."

"Yes, I wonder!" Janine enthused.

An hour or so after breakfast, the groom and best man came downstairs. Janine's eyes nearly popped out of her head when she saw them, resplendent in their grey morning suits, a simple yellow rose in each lapel. They were being picked up and driven to the church in ten minutes and were looking expectantly down the drive.

"Oh wow! you look great," Janine gushed.

"Thanks," they answered in unison, admitting they felt a bit nervous.

"So long as I've got the ring, we'll be fine," the best man laughed, shaking the girls' hands. "I'm Ivan by the way. Thanks for a great breakfast."

"Yes, it was very good, thank you." interjected the groom, as he checked the time anxiously on his watch.

"Don't worry dear, we're ready now," Mrs Blake

trilled, as she and Mr Blake came down the stairs in their wedding finery.

"Oh wow," Holly and Janine cooed, "You all look gorgeous."

"Hang on a minute," Holly said, running back into the kitchen and grabbing her phone to take a picture.

"I just love weddings," Janine squealed.
As they all chatted politely, with Janine still 'oohing' and 'ahhing' at the happy spectacle, a silver-grey, vintage Bentley purred up the drive.

"Time to go," Ivan said, thoroughly in control of the situation, as he patted his friend protectively on the back before ushering him and his parents towards the door.

"OMG he's lovely," Janine swooned.

"Think he has the eye for you," Holly whispered, "Better start using your journalistic skills and find out if he is single."

"See you later ladies," Ivan called back, as he held the car door open for Mr and Mrs Blake.

"See you later," the girls replied.

"Ooh I think I need a brandy," Holly remarked wistfully.

"Me too." added Janine.

"They looked so happy, didn't they?" Janine said swirling her brandy.

"They certainly have the wow factor," Holly agreed, trying to imagine Mac, dressed so beautifully, proclaiming to the world that Holly was the one and only woman for him.
The two girls drank their brandy in reflective silence then polished off a packet of shortbread biscuits.

"I'll do Ivan's room," Janine insisted.

"You want to poke around, see if Mr gorgeous is single!"

"Holly, how could you suggest such a thing? It never crossed my mind," Janine answered cheekily, before disappearing into his room with Madge's cleaning box.

"Nice clothes," she giggled, coming downstairs carrying a collection of wet towels. "C'mon!" she said, putting down Madge's cleaning box, "Let's go and see them throwing the confetti."

"Janine! You are a glutton for punishment!" But Holly gave in, it was a lovely morning, Tess needed a walk and the church was near the fields.

They hung around, tucked behind a hedge in the churchyard waiting for the happy couple to come out. The church organist was playing "The Toccata" as a beaming bride and groom walked proudly out of the church. Family and friends then followed out into the beautiful June sunshine, confetti at the ready. All the men were in morning dress and the ladies wore some spectacular hats. The bride was radiant. Her tiara glinted in the sunshine while her long blonde hair was neatly swept up into a falling cascade of curls. Her hand tucked neatly into her new husband's arm, the couple smiled, posed and kissed for the cameras under an array of fragrant, falling rose petals.

"Well, I'm always the bridesmaid and never the bride," Janine remarked wistfully, "I wonder if he's single" she added, looking longingly at Ivan.

"I can't see anyone with him," Holly said, in an encouraging tone. "You'd better get in quick, he's off tomorrow." Then linking arms with her friend and letting Tess off the lead, she said: "I think Mrs Blake said some of the wedding party would be in the pub tonight so we can always pop over for a drink."

"Oohh yes, let's," said Janine visibly brightening.

After a nice afternoon, shopping in Chichester, they went over to the 'Bulls Head' for a chicken and chips supper. Janine didn't need any persuading. Sure enough, an hour to two later the wedding guests flocked in looking flushed and happy.

"Hi, how did everything go?" Holly asked Ivan as she was buying Janine and herself a large glass of red wine.

"Terrific, it's been a perfect day. Let me buy you ladies a drink to say thank you for the lovely break-fasts," and before Holly could argue, he had paid for their drinks.

"The gentleman insists," Paul, the landlord, joked surreptitiously, winking at Holly and pushing her card away, as Ivan invited Holly and Janine to join the rest of the party over in the corner of the pub. Mr Blake was holding court telling funny stories about the Groom growing up.

Yasmin and Dan were both newly qualified doctors and despite being part of such a glamorous party, they only had eyes for one another. Dan hung on every word Yasmin uttered. They were going to get the train back to London later that night but Ivan had mentioned that he was staying in Willow Cottage and so, apologising for not making a booking earlier, they asked Holly if they could stay too.

"I've got eleven rooms free so that isn't a problem," She joked.

Before they knew it, it was last orders. Paul clanged the bell at the bar and after much backslapping and air-kissing amongst new-found friends in the pub, Holly, Janine, and the wedding party traipsed back to Willow Cottage.

Yasmin and Dan loved the house and were thrilled to be staying in the Lavender Room. After bringing in their cases Holly brought out the bottle of champagne she'd bought to share with Mac, then fetched her crystal champagne glasses and proposed a toast to the happy couple. Janine and Ivan were clearly enjoying getting to know one another better, so winking at her friend, Holly made her excuses and went to bed, taking Tess with her for company. Checking her mobile, before snuggling exhausted into bed, she saw there wasn't any message from Mac.

Oh well, at least I've got a lie in tomorrow. No one wanted breakfast until ten. Mr Wainwright had gone home for the weekend and Stuart was in London.

So who will be making your breakfast tomorrow Mr Perone? Holly wondered as she changed the time of her alarm call.

"Oh, I don't want to go back to London,' Janine wailed into her coffee after her long lingering good bye to Ivan the next day. Mr and Mrs Blake, Yasmin and Dan had left an hour or so before and Janine and Ivan had taken Tess for a walk over the fields after breakfast. Holly could see she was clearly smitten with him and the attraction appeared to be mutual.

"I'm going to end it with Jim." Janine said decisively.

Holly didn't want to put a damper on her getting together with Ivan, but pointed out that Yorkshire was a long way from London, so maybe she shouldn't pin all her hopes on someone who lived so far away.

"I know," Janine agreed stirring her coffee, "But things can't be right between Jim and me if I can feel this attraction to someone else, can they?"

Holly agreed, thinking of Stuart.

"He said he'd call me," Janine said, going all little girly and studying his card.

"I'm sure he will," said Holly, "He seems really genuine, not like the 'fly-by-night' media types you and I usually meet. Speaking of which, Mac hasn't called, he said he'd come down tonight but I bet he won't" she remarked flatly as she poured them more coffee from her cafeteria.

"Time to move on Hol," Janine said brightly, "Out with the old and in with the new."

Chapter Eight

The house seemed eerily quiet after the departure of the wedding guests, so it was great that Janine said she could stay for an extra night. They were just dozing off in front of the television, with Tess at their feet when the phone rang. It was Mac.

"I'm so sorry I didn't make it down babe, I just got so caught up with this bloody pitch. Haven't even shaved."

"Oh, don't worry," Holly answered coolly. "Janine's here and I had a delightful wedding party staying." She knew from the reaction, or lack of one, that he wasn't really listening, so when the doorbell rang, Holly was pleased to cut the conversation short.

Just as she opened her door someone leapt out of the bushes to the side of her house and snapped a picture of her.

"Is Stuart Perone staying here?" they demanded.

"Yes, he is" Holly snapped back. "What's this all about?"

"He's just won the Goodwood Racing cup," He said. "You a close friend?"

"Janine!" Holly called out, as she shut the door and turned back into the dining room.

"It's the bloody paparazzi. They're after Stuart. One's just snapped a picture of me. He's won the Goodwood Cup."

"Blimey, it all happens in Willow Cottage," Janine remarked, putting down her cup of tea and getting up to peek out of the window.

"He must be a real celeb... Hol, I'll have to get an interview."

"You'd be crazy not to," Holly agreed. "I'll have a word, see what I can set up for you. C'mon let's go to the pub, see what we can find out."

Grabbing their handbags, they marched purposefully down the path, past the assembled photographers and into the 'Bulls Head'.

"Did you watch Stuart race today? Are you close friends?" they called out.

"No, we didn't watch him race today but we may do tomorrow." Janine answered, batting her eyelashes as they flashed their cameras.

"God. I thought this was the quiet life," Holly remarked as they sat down with their drinks in a cosy corner of the pub.

"Margery would love this!" Janine smiled. "Two, seasoned, London journalists chased into a country pub by a gang of baying photographers! This doesn't happen to us in London…"

"I know… and they've got my bloody picture. Don't know why."

The Bulls Head was a typical old English country pub, which, like Willow Cottage dated back to the sixteenth century. Copper pans and pictures of hunting scenes adorned the walls and a huge open fireplace dominated the lounge.

"Oh, I could live in the country." Janine remarked admiring the surroundings.

Stuart and his entourage spilled into the pub just as the girls were relaxing with their drinks. The women looked elegant in their elaborate hats, killer-heels and clingy dresses.

He didn't look in a very good mood as he went to the bar.

"Ooh looks as if something's ruffled his feathers," remarked Holly. *He's just won his race, the misery guts…"

Congregating around the bar, Stuart's entourage were clearly in the mood to celebrate. A very pretty, dark-haired, Hispanic looking girl nestled closer to Stuart, hanging on to every word he spoke. Just as Holly was watching them, he spotted her at her table with Janine. A delicious electric shock thrilled though her body as their eyes locked. Embarrassed, she immediately looked away.

"You alright Hol?" Janine asked, noticing her friends flushed cheeks.

Ooh he's coming over...

"Did you know anything about the photographers outside your house?" He asked in an accusatory tone, fixing Holly with a stare.

"No, I didn't." she answered truthfully.

He didn't look convinced.

"Congratulations on winning the race. I'm Janine O'Leary, one of Holly's old colleagues from '*Smile*' Magazine."

Great. Now he'll think I set him up.

"If you wanted an interview, you just had to ask." He told them, his deep, dark eyes boring into Holly's embarrassed gaze.

"Stuart, believe me, those photographers had nothing to do with us."

He shrugged his shoulders.

"Please ladies, join us, we are in the mood to celebrate."

"Great. C'mon Hol," Janine nudged Holly. Embarrassed and a little confused, Holly quietly followed her over to Stuart's table. The champagne was flowing while the dark-haired girl constantly eyed Holly and Janine, trying her best to keep Stuart captive with her ridiculous pouts. She clearly wasn't happy that two more pretty women were joining the group and her ridiculous and incessant laughing clearly didn't just annoy Holly and Janine.

Holly had to get up, cook breakfast and make beds for another four guests in the morning, but Janine was clearly having a great time and Holly didn't want to spoil her fun. She was going through a hard time. Margery had given everyone a rollicking that week. A new rival magazine had come out and *'Smile'* was fighting to keep its place on the shelves. Janine had to get a story out of Stuart.

"We're going back for a party at Goodwood House. Would you like to join us?" he asked Holly, edging away from the dark-haired beauty and slipping in the space between her and Janine. She could feel the heat from his body and his taught muscular thigh so close to her own, sent a shiver down her spine.

"I promise I won't mention the car, or you moving me out of my room," He said, teasingly, pushing his thick, dark wavy hair back from his handsome forehead.

Janine was frantically mouthing "Yes!" and nodding her head behind him, so Holly agreed they'd go.

"We'll be back in a minute," Holly said grabbing Janine by her arm. "We've got to get changed," she whispered in her ear. "It's a stately house, everyone will be dressed up to the nines."

"Omg Hol, what am I going to wear? I didn't bring anything down."

"Something of mine," Holly laughed, rattling the key in the lock in her haste to get into the house.

"It's okay Tess everything is fine," Holly called back to the dog as she followed them up the stairs.

Twenty or so minutes later, Holly had transformed herself from country girl to sophisticated girl about town. She was wearing an electric blue, silk sheath dress that molded itself around her body, leaving nothing to the male imagination. Her hair expertly swept up in a French style chignon and the highest heels she could walk in. Janine slipped into an equally figure-hugging, lime green velvet dress and pair of Holly's black Christian Louboutin shoes.

Heads turned as the two girls walked back into the pub. Stuart's eyes feasted on Holly the moment she came in.

Their convoy of cars snaked through the fabulous gates and grounds of Goodwood house. Thousands of fairy lights lit up the tree-lined entrance to the party. Young, good-looking PR types ticked off names from the guest list at the huge oak doors leading into the stately home.

"How's he going to get us in?" Janine whispered to Holly, "There's a guest list."

"God knows, down to him," Holly answered, only really bothered in case Janine was disappointed. But two extra good-looking girls didn't seem to be a problem and they were waved in. It was a fabulous party, with a live band, acrobatic displays and wall to wall video coverage of the days racing with a close-up of Stuart, kissing his trophy, which he held aloft his handsome head, to the cheering crowd.

Champagne and free drinks were flowing. Janine was having a great time dancing with Henrik, one of his team of mechanics. Then the music was sultry and sexy and Holly found herself relaxing. Happy to 'People-watch' as she quietly sipped her champagne. The dark-haired beauty spent most of the night hanging around Stuart's neck, slurring her words and stumbling across the dance floor, but he was a perfect gentleman, appearing to take it all in his stride.

Then, just as a particularly sensual number came up he sauntered over to Holly.

"Come along Miss Bradbury, you are dancing with me," he said decisively, pulling her up and leading her over to the dance floor. Holding her close she could feel his breath on her neck, as his hands gently pushed her body closer to his. Soon they were swaying tenderly to Marvin Gaye's hit '*Let's make love tonight.*'

"Relax," he whispered in her ear, "The night is young, all too soon you will have that apron on..."
As the music ended, he led her gently by her hand onto the balcony which was festooned with fairy lights and shady, palm trees. *What's a beautiful girl like you doing cooped up in a huge house on her own? he mused. You're irresistible...*

"Come let's walk," he said, leading her down the balcony steps to the sculpted gardens. "I want to get to know you."
He was surprisingly easy to talk to but he could sense that Holly was holding back. She wasn't about to tell him the real reason she came to be at Willow Cottage and cleverly side-tracked his questions. So, slipping into journalistic mode she asked him about his racing.

"I only ever wanted to race cars, my poor parents were very disappointed, they had hoped I'd be a doctor."

"But they must be so proud..."

"Maybe, but it isn't much fun for my mother watching me dice with death on the track, but that's what we do. That's the thrill and we are only as good as our last race. That's hard for a mother."
Overpowered by the urge to kiss her, he pulled her towards him and she didn't resist. His hands, expertly pulled the pins out of her hair which fell down her back in long, chestnut-brown tendrils. Then they moved expertly over her breasts as she hungrily reciprocated his kiss, pulling him roughly towards her. She could feel

him pressing against her as they both fought for breath between each greedy kiss.

"Oh god, please, Stuart please, stop."

"Okay, Okay," he said kissing her neck. "Let's go back in and join the party."

Holly could feel his eyes on her the whole time they were there. "I'm going to get to know you a lot better Holly Bradbury," he whispered into her ear.

"Are you now?" she teased him back.

"Yes," he answered tipping her chin up for a kiss. The pretty dark-haired girl had latched on to another tall, dark handsome party go-er and Janine was dancing as if there was no tomorrow.

Around three am, the party started to break up. Stuart accompanied Holly and Janine back to Willow Cottage in one of the waiting cars. The two girls resting their sleepy heads on his broad, muscular shoulders.

After they had said good night to Janine, Stuart caught Holly at the top of the stairs near his room. Pushing her against the wall, they had a long sumptuous kiss as his body pushed harder and harder against her. Then he scooped her up into his strong muscular arms and carried her into his room where he laid her gently on the bed.

"Stay, stay with me," he whispered in her ear as he removed her shoes, sensually stroking and kissing the sole of her foot. His sensual mouth travelling up over her toes, her calves, her knees then up her inner thigh. Just as Holly wound her legs around him, his phone rang. The moment had gone. Annoyed, he picked up the call and Holly could hear it was a woman.

As she went to move off the bed and make for the door, he caught her arm, trying to get her to stay.

Shaking him off, she picked up her shoes and left the

room. She'd just got to her door, when she heard him behind her.

"Holly," he said, "It's not what you think," his eyes were pleading with her.

Furious, she slammed the door in his face.

You can't and will not fall for him, Holly Bradbury, she repeated to herself as she stomped up and down her bedroom. Tess, eyed her mistress sleepily as she continued pacing up and down.

"He has a girl at every race, doesn't he Tess?" she said, stroking her behind her ear. "Looks like you and I are going to be sharing a room for a while."

Chapter Nine

It was nine o'clock and Holly and Janine were in the kitchen fighting over the aspirin. Holly was expecting some Spanish guests to come down for breakfast.

"Oh, please god they don't have a fried breakfast, I don't think I could stand it." Janine wailed. Holly didn't feel much better, but soldiered on. Getting sausages, eggs and bacon out of the fridge in preparation.

"Phew, they just want coffee and toast." Janine said coming back in from the dining room.

"Yes!" Holly punched the air. "Now we've just got Stuart."

But he didn't come down.

He was probably sleeping. Should I take him up some coffee and waffles? Holly could imagine his taught muscular body, sprawled over the bed, ooh it was so tempting to get the master-key to his room and slide in next to him, the weight of his body on top of her, his hands in her hair, snaking down towards her breasts, his hot breath in her ear, little bites of pleasure over her stomach and hips…

Once the Spanish guests had exited the dining room, Janine made some long-awaited coffee.

"You look a million miles away."

"I am," Holly smiled, thanking her for the coffee and taking a sip.

"So, should we go and wake up your delicious racing driver? You two were getting on very well last night…"

"He'll have a woman at every race. I'm not going to be another notch on his bedpost." Holly tried to sound nonchalant.

Just as the girls were sipping their coffee, the doorbell rang and Tess bounded to the door, Holly in tow. It was the infuriating dark-haired beauty from Stuart's entourage. She looked a lot younger and even prettier without her make-up and was dressed simply in jeans and a jumper.

"Hi," she said, without any of the previous night's bravado, "Is Stuart there?"
Before Holly could answer, she heard his familiar steps coming down the stairs.

"Hi," he greeted her casually completely by-passing Holly.

"C'mon let's go out and get some coffee," he said putting a protective arm around her shoulders. "Are you feeling better this morning?"
Holly looked on miserably as they made their way down the garden path.
He barely acknowledged me, brazenly invites another woman to my house then goes out for a coffee with her. Thank God we didn't spend the night together.
Holly was furious.

"Sorry Hol, I'm going back to bed for a bit, my heads killing me." Janine cut in as she came out of the dining room and saw them disappearing down the garden path.

"Who was that?"

"Tell you later," Holly answered flatly. "Get your head down and thanks so much for helping me"

"Yes, think I will," Janine said, pecking her friend on the cheek. "You should too, we didn't get much sleep last night."

"Good idea," Holly answered intending to do just that. But just as she was making her way to her room, the phone rang. It was Mac.

"I'm really sorry I didn't get down Hol. Been working all weekend on this bloody pitch... should be able to make it next weekend. Thought I'd come with Jonathan, my mate from the gym. He says there's some great windsurfing just up the road from you at the Witterings. Strictly business of course, we don't want any special favours and we'll pay the going rate."
No, he bloody well wouldn't get any favours and yes, they would be paying the going rate - for a twin room!
If she'd had the energy Holly would have told him to go to hell but her head hurt too much. *Oh god! I'm going to jump into bed and shut out the world.*

A couple of hours later, the girls were awake and refreshed, enjoying a last cup of tea together in the dining room before Janine's drive back to London.
"He's checking up on you Holly," Janine said authoritively. "Why else would he come down? He must have put his friend up to the windsurfing idea so he could see you."
Maybe he did. But what the hell.
Even though she didn't want to admit it to herself, Holly was intrigued.
As Janine, bound for London Town, tooted goodbye in her Mini Cooper, Holly felt engulfed by a horrible wave of what she now recognised as loneliness.

***

Mac and Jonathan arrived around seven the following Friday night, with copious bottles of wine and beer. Handing her a beautiful bunch of hand-tied flowers, Mac held her in his arms a moment or two longer than one would normally do for a casual, friendly greeting.
"You look great Hol, he said looking into her eyes. The country air suits you."

He looked pretty good himself, but then he always did with his youthful blonde, blue-eyed, Adonis good looks. Holly liked his friend, Jonathan, whom she hadn't met before. He was interested in the house and clearly admired her entrepreneurial spirit. While Mac busied himself putting the beer and wine in the fridge and fetching glasses, Holly gave Jonathan a quick tour of the house. Mac caught them up as Holly was showing Jonathan into their twin room.

But Mac was more taken with the Passion-flower Room.

"I take it this is for us then Hol," he laughed as Holly showed them her best room with the prize four poster bed.

"This is the marital suite," she laughed, "You know, when people make things legal!"

"Think Holly's trying to tell you something mate," Jonathan laughed.

"Yes, it's the twin for you matey," Holly teased patting his stomach playfully.

"Think you've been neglecting the gym Mac, or, don't tell me - You've been existing on takeaways." Mac pretended to look hurt but had to admit since Holly's departure his eating habits hadn't been good.

"C'mon, let's get a drink and check out that pub."

"Sounds good to me," Jonathan agreed, but he was a sensitive guy, and appreciated their need to be alone. "Just going to have a quick shower, see you there."

"You are indeed a woman of property." Mac remarked fondly, "It's gorgeous Holly."

"Glad you like it."

"It's good that you got a dog," he interjected protectively.

"I didn't have a choice really, the Baxters weren't going to take her with them. She's a great guard dog, I do feel safer with her around... See you later darling."

Holly said, giving Tess a chew and shutting her in the sitting room. She didn't want her intimidating her other guests if they came back while they were out.

Then, grabbing their coats they made their way to the pub.

"Hiya Holly," Paul, the manager, who ran the pub with his delightful wife, Dawn, greeted her cheerfully at the bar. "How's business?"

"Good," Holly answered, brightly introducing Mac. The barmaids, Holly noticed were looking at him approvingly.

"Holly's doing very well," Dawn said. "Apparently her breakfasts are vastly superior to the Baxters.'

Holly's eyes lit up.

"No, really?"

"Yes, really, word gets around here like wildfire." Jonathan came into the pub as Mac carried their drinks to a secluded table in the corner, Holly was on cloud nine.

"Apparently my breakfasts are better than the previous owners." She proudly told Jonathan as he joined them at their table.

Just as they were demolishing their drinks, Holly spotted Stuart and the dark-haired girl sitting across the pub from them. They were giggling and looking at her tablet. Her heart sank at the sight of them. But then her sensible head took over. *What got into me last night? I would have stayed the night with him if he hadn't got that phone call.*

"Holly, are you with us or them?" Mac chided her, putting his arm possessively around her.

"Oh sorry, just spotted one of my guests."

Mac was more interested in telling Holly and Jonathan about the new account he'd just won.

Stuart hadn't spotted her and Holly couldn't help staring as he gallantly held the door for that infuriating girl. But just as they were leaving he caught Holly's eye.

"See you tomorrow around eight?" he called over, his eyes boring into her.

"Yes, yes that's fine. One egg or two?"
Mac looked at her as if she was bonkers while Jonathan suppressed a smile.
But Stuart hadn't heard her. Holly could see through the window he was too busy hugging the girl before she went off in a taxi.
A moment later, she watched him cross the road and walk up the path to Willow Cottage. Her heart was beating in her ears as she fought the urge to chase after him.

Holly did relent. Mac didn't sleep in the twin room with Jonathan. She and Mac slept in the four-poster room. Fuelled by the wine, she gave in to his charms and it was nice to wake up with his familiar bulk next to her. But the earth didn't move and it was Stuart Perone she was thinking about rather than Mac. *Who was that girl? He wasn't interested in her at the party but then why did she turn up at the house this morning? They must have spent the day together. And they were so intimately engrossed in looking at her tablet...*

Checking her watch, she saw that it was nearly half past seven and she had to cook Stuart breakfast at eight, so just had time to rush down and tackle the snail slime. Mac clearly had other things on his mind and tried to pull her back into bed. Resisting his charms, she showered and got dressed. Then, tucking her hair up into a neat chignon, she applied an expert line of eye-liner.

Mac was watching her at the mirror, a look of yearning in his eyes. She was just applying her trade mark, cherry-red lipstick when he leapt out of bed and pressed his hard, naked body against hers. His strong, familiar muscular arms pulling her close.

"Stay Hol, I've missed you," he whispered in her ear.

But Holly wasn't tempted. Planting a peck on his cheek she made her way to the door, smoothing her skirt.

"No breakfast after nine," she smiled, quietly closing the door behind her.

She was cooking some sausages and bacon when she heard Stuart's now familiar steps coming down the stairs. Making his way into the dining room, she busied herself getting his coffee. He's late. Had he sneaked her in to his room last night? Maybe he'd gone back to her hotel then returned to Willow Cottage in the early hours?

Holly could feel his eyes on her as she brought in his breakfast.

"Nice pub," he said brightly, pouring his coffee, "The food is very good."

They were politely discussing the merits of the Bulls Head when Mac and Jonathan came into the dining room. Mac made a big thing of calling Holly 'darling' and kissing her on her cheek in front of Stuart. Holly could have killed him. Stuart quietly took in the scene, politely saying good morning while stirring his coffee. Holly introduced Mac and Jonathan as 'her friends from London.'

"I'm Holly's *close* friend." Mac corrected her, vigorously buttering his neatly cut triangle of toast. Holly felt her cheeks burn as she turned back into the sanctity of her kitchen to bring out more coffee.

Mr and Mrs Jones, a charming Welsh couple, were in the dining room now and Holly was busy juggling the timings of hot toast, tea, coffee and eggs and bacon cooked to perfection. She felt acutely embarrassed serving her guests under Mac and Jonathan's watchful eyes, but they were now tucking heartily into their own full English breakfasts.

Stuart was checking his tablet at his table. Five minutes or so later, he waved Holly good-bye, wished Mac and Jonathan a good day, picked up his keys and made his way out the front door, reminding Holly that tonight would be the last night he was staying.

"He a regular?" Mac asked, an edge of possessiveness in his voice.

The boys had clearly enjoyed their breakfast. Jonathan thoughtfully took their plates out to the kitchen and started stacking them in the dishwasher while Mac buttered more toast. Holly told Jonathan not to worry but he insisted all the same, even taking out her guests' dishes.

"Now that's quite enough," Holly joked, chasing him from the dining room with the rolling pin she was given by her colleagues at the magazine.

Still laughing, she sat down at Mac's table and helped herself to his coffee and left-over toast.

"I miss you Hol," Mac said, taking her hand in his across the table. Holly's stomach flipped as her eyes burned into the white linen table cloth. She wished he hadn't said that and didn't know what to say.

"Do you miss me?" He persisted.

Holly felt a lump in her throat and for once, was stuck for words. The air was heavy with the silence between them.

"I don't know Mac. Yes, maybe, sometimes... It's good to see you," she said quickly, putting her hand on top of his, "It really is."

Emotion and unspoken words hung heavily in the air.

"I'd better get on," she said getting up from the table, "I've got to do the rooms."
She was shaken by Mac's vulnerability around her. He had always been the one calling the shots in their relationship. Blinded by her obsession with him, Holly could be quite weak around him, often, according to Janine *'Melting into a meek little woman in his presence.'* Her loud, at times, brash, great hulk of a man was showing a side she didn't know existed. The man who never said he loved her, even in their most intimate moments had now said he missed her and that his life wasn't the same without her.

Despite the initial awkwardness between them, it had been a good weekend. The boys had gone wind-surfing and they'd all enjoyed some fabulous strolls along the beach at West Witterings with Tess. Mac and Jonathan loved the friendly village pubs and agreed to come back to the 'Bulls Head' monthly jazz night later that month.
But as Mac's Mazda crunched its way down the drive bound for London and their old home, Holly was overtaken by loneliness again, and for a moment she wanted to jump in the seat next to him. Had her miscarriage made her bitter and twisted? Would she be alone cooking eggs and bacon and sweating over a hot iron for the rest of her life? Playing Auntie to all her friends' children, like Auntie Maud?
Tears smudged her mascara as she made her way back inside the house. It was so quiet. So big and empty. Making herself a coffee she snuggled into Tess's huge bulky frame, closed her eyes and relived those fabulous intimate moments.
With Stuart.

The rest of the day passed in a miserable blur. Stuart was leaving the next day and thanks to Mac's little performance, that would probably be the last she ever saw of him. Holly went to bed ridiculously early with a good book, in the desperate hope that she could shut out all thoughts of her irresistible racing driver. It wasn't long until she fell into a fitful sleep but woke up with a start, when she saw it was midnight on her digital bedside clock.

Setting her alarm for seven she snuggled under the covers and tried to go to back to sleep; banishing any wicked thoughts she harboured about Stuart from her brain; but then a high pitched, piercing screech cut through the silence of the night.

"My god! The Bugatti!" She called out to herself, "Quick Tess, let's go."

Tess didn't need any encouragement, barking loudly, she bounded two at a time, down the stairs after Holly into the night.

The security lights flashed on as Holly raced down the drive towards the garage. To her horror she saw a man trying to open the garage door with a crowbar.

"Get back Holly! Get back! - leave this to me!" Stuart shouted as he ran down the path after her. Launching himself at the man, they wrestled madly in the fluorescent beams of the security lights. Then two gunshots rang through the air as the man, wearing a Balaklava and brandishing a gun, broke away from Stuart and ran away into the fields behind the garage. There was a loud yelp as Tess slunk to the ground. Holly's blood froze as she collapsed over Tess's seemingly lifeless body.

"Tess! Tess! darling!" She wailed as Stuart knelt beside her. She was aware of his calming voice but couldn't focus on a word he was saying through her tears.

Within minutes, a police car alerted by the alarm sped up the drive, blue lights flashing. Stuart calmly took control of the situation telling the officers what had happened while Holly went back into the house to get a blanket for Tess. As they took Holly's statement Stuart contacted a veterinary hospital and following their instructions, tenderly covered the whimpering Tess with the blanket. As they were talking to the police, a vet arrived to examine her. After administering a pain-killer, Stuart helped him lift Tess onto a stretcher and into the back of the vet's car. She would need surgery to remove the bullets. Holly couldn't contain her tears and was desperate to go with Tess but the vet gently but firmly dissuaded her from going.

"There nothing you can do and it will be very stressful for you. We will keep you posted. It's best you stay at home."

As the vet drove off Stuart pulled her close and let her weep into his broad chest. Then guiding her gently back into the house, he found some brandy and poured them both a drink. The fire of the amber liquid jolted Holly back to reality.

"My gentle giant," she murmured. "My gentle, gentle giant..."

"She will be okay. She's in good hands." Stuart tried to assure her. She was so glad he was there. She couldn't have coped being alone. But then she remembered, he had seen off the thief.

"My god Stuart, are you okay, are you hurt?"

"I'm fine."

"You are not, look!" she exclaimed in shock, spotting the long gash on his forearm. "Here, let me at least wash it," she said, going to get her first aid box from the cupboard under the stairs. She could feel his eyes on her as she gently tended his wound.

"I think we should go to A&E," Holly said concerned.

"No," Stuart said decisively, pouring them both another brandy.

I've been in enough scrapes to know that this is just a superficial cut. You've done a great job, Nurse Bradbury."

"Yes, but…"

"No buts, I'm fine. Now let's have a drink."

"Thank you so much Stuart, he had a gun, when I think what could have happened…" Holly put her head in her hands, "And all for a stupid car. You could have been killed…"

"Well, I couldn't have you accusing me, if it went," he smiled, taking her hand.

The next thing she knew, he had scooped her up in his arms and was carrying her purposefully upstairs to his room. How she wanted him on top of her… Inside her. Only his making love to her could banish this awful pain. But he didn't touch her. Just gently laid her on the bed and smoothed her hair back from her tear-stained face before switching off the light and closing the door.

"You need to sleep Holly. Tess will be okay and the car is fine."

Drifting off to sleep she dreamt that Stuart was racing the Bugatti along the empty shores of a golden West Sussex beach. Holly in the front beside him and Tess in the back. Just the three of them.

Chapter Ten

She woke up late the next morning in an empty bed. Stuart had left a note on her bedside table.

Holly,
You have had a shock and I didn't want to wake you.
The vet phoned to say that Tess had a good night. As you know I am leaving today and so have left my key and the money I owe you inside the ceramic chicken in your kitchen.
Take it easy Princess.
Stuart.
X

Stuart was leaving today and her beloved dog wasn't even with her. Choking back tears, Holly called the veterinary hospital. The kindly nurse, gently informed her that Tess was in theatre having two bullets removed from her chest. Holly could come in later that day after the surgery. As she put down the phone, Holly forced herself to get on with her day. Putting on the radio she tried to settle down to clear a mounting mound of ironing when the phone rang. It was Janine.

"Guess what Hol? I'm going to see Ivan next week. We've been speaking most nights on the phone since the wedding and he's invited me up to stay for a few days next week."

"Oh, Janine that's great, I'm so pleased for you. I take it things are off with Jim then?"

"Yes, I think he was happy I was the one to end things… what's up, you don't sound yourself this morning?"

Holly burst into tears then blurted out the sorry tale of Tess, the near theft of the Bugatti and Stuart's injury.

"God, it was awful," Holly wailed down the phone in between ironing a duvet-cover that just wouldn't lose its crinkles. "I just broke down in front of him!"

"Yeah, but it made you closer..." Janine tried to comfort her friend.

"It was good to be held in his arms – but not as a snivelling bloody wreck." *Oh god it's too embarrassing to think about.*

"Have you heard from Mac?" Janine interjected gently.

"He called from work, thanking me for the weekend. Apparently, Jonathan loved the house and will be coming down regularly for the windsurfing, which I'm hoping will be good for business as he's got lots of surfing friends."

"So?" Janine probed...

"What?" Holly asked, confused.

"Did you give in? Did Mac sneak into your room?" Holly didn't want to answer but knew Janine would guess.

"I bloody well gave in."

"Holly!" Janine feigned shock, "You said he was going in the twin!"

"That's what I intended, but the wine got the better of me, besides... I did miss him."

"You were together a long time, it's hard just to cut off."

Holly was touched by her friend's generosity of spirit because she knew it was a backward step to sleep with Mac, although she had to concede, she'd been lonely and missed his familiar touch and manly presence.

"I know there'll be another girl somewhere soon, Mac can't cope for long without a girlfriend."

Janine went quiet for a moment.

"I didn't want to tell you this Hol, but a young girl at his office fancies him. Margery saw them together in a wine bar. Apparently, the girl looked a lot more interested than Mac, and when Margery spoke to him, she said he seemed a bit down, and confessed to missing you.

Now Holly was more confused than ever.

Why then hadn't he pleaded with her to stay in London? It wasn't as if he stopped her packing her cases! For god's sake, if ever there was a time to tell her he loved her it was then! He must have seen how upset she was. It was a major decision giving up her career, swapping her London life for one in the country and completely on her own, to boot!

But looking back Holly reflected, he was more upset about her giving up her so-called 'glamorous' job at 'Smile.' Cooking eggs and bacon in the country clearly wasn't as impressive. He had to have a girlfriend he could show off; who did "*Something in the media*," wore stilettoes and bright red lipstick. Holly would have liked to chat longer but the reality of Janine chasing deadlines cut their conversation short.

Fury suddenly surged in Holly's veins as she unplugged the iron. She had to get out. To hell with everything and everyone. And she was sick of ironing sheets! She'd go riding. She needed to gallop through some fields, feel the wind in her hair, the sun on her face.

Picking up her mobile, she checked out a local riding stable then left a note for Madge, telling her which rooms to do.

***

"Misty should be fine for you Miss," said Mr Johnson, the wizened old farmer who owned the local stables, "She's a bit feisty, but if you say you are an experienced rider you should be alright."

Patting the chestnut Arab on her soft nose, Holly assured him that she would be fine. She wanted to ride a horse with spirit. The Last time she'd been riding was in Richmond Park in London, when she was recovering from her miscarriage; it was an instant "de-stress" and just what Holly needed now to take her mind off everything.

Swinging her leg expertly over the saddle, she tucked her feet into the stirrups, pulled the reins, and directed Misty towards the open country. It was a beautiful morning; the sun was dappling through the leaves on the chestnut trees in the rolling West Sussex countryside. Riding a horse, Holly re-assured herself, was like riding a bicycle. You never really forget; you may be rusty to start but it soon came back. After a gentle trot, they moved into a canter then a full gallop across the velvety green fields. Misty was in her element and the faster and harder her hooves pounded the ground, the calmer Holly felt; her frustrations and worries disappearing with every lunge the horse made.

"That be quite a workout young Miss." said Mr Johnson patting Misty's forelock when they returned an hour or so later. Both the horse and Holly were breathing hard after their exertions.

"It was wonderful, thank you Mr. Johnson, just what I need to take my mind off things."

Holly then proceeded to tell the attentive old man about Tess being shot.

"You take care now young Miss, you are a fine rider, and give that dog a pat from me."

"I will." Holly said as she settled-up and made her way back to her car.

Just as she was making her way up to the house she was confronted by a lady at the front door carrying a huge bunch of flowers.

"Are you Miss Holly Bradbury?" she asked. "There you go luv."

Thanking her profusely, Holly made her way into the dining room. It was an impressive bouquet of jasmine, roses and lilies, hand-tied and free-standing in its own cellophane vase. The scent from the lilies was intoxicating. Taking out the card, Holly saw they were from Stuart.

'Just a little something to cheer you up. Very sorry you were so upset,
Stuart X.'

Holly's heart was in her mouth. Hugging his card to her heart she did a little dance round her dining room. Her instinct was to rush to the phone and tell Janine but she knew she'd be in a features meeting. Holly felt seventeen again. *I'll have to phone him up and thank him. But no, not the second I get them. How sad would that look?*

"They be a fine bouquet," Madge said, impressed. From your young gentleman in London, are they?" she asked, smelling a rose.

"Actually, they are from our racing driver. He knew I was upset about Tess so..."

Madge had noticed that Tess wasn't in the house as soon as she arrived that morning and was as upset as Holly when she heard what happened.

"Oh, Holly! How lovely. He sent you flowers! Now that be a fine thing to do..."

"Yes, a fine thing," Holly agreed, a blush tinging her cheeks.

The phone rang just as Holly had made coffee for the two of them. It was the veterinary hospital. Tess had her operation and the bullets had been successfully removed. Luckily, they were from an air pistol rather than a real gun.

Holly burst into tears as soon as she got off the phone. Madge did the same. Not knowing what to do with themselves, Holly suggested they go together to the hospital. Madge didn't need any encouragement. Putting on her coat, she retrieved a dog biscuit from her battered pocket.

"Do you think she'd be allowed her bissie dear?" As much as they tried to control themselves, both Holly and Madge burst into tears when they saw Tess. The poor old girl, feebly wagged her tail when she heard their voices and tried to sit up but she was so weak she could hardly lift her head.

"There, there, darling, you will be okay." Holly soothed her.

Madge sheepishly put the dog biscuit back in her pocket as the nurse told them that Tess wasn't allowed to eat.

"You'll be home soon darling." Madge added, a quake in her voice as they were leaving.

Wiping away a tear, Holly was incredibly grateful that she had Madge there with her for support.

"I hope she is home soon Madge, life would be unbearable without my protector."

"She will be dear," Madge said kindly, "You'll be home soon won't you Tess?" Tess wagged her tail. "There you see, she's telling you she will."

Linking arms, the two women walked slowly out of the surgery and back to Holly's car. Madge kindly asked Holly in for a cup of tea when she dropped her home but knew Madge's mother could be cantankerous and often embarrassed Madge in front of guests, so Holly made her excuses.

The house felt incredibly empty. Holly checked Stuart's room in the vain hope that he would be there but of course he wasn't.

Later that evening, feeling nervous and with a generous glass of white wine for courage Holly dialled the number he registered with when he checked in to Willow Cottage. After two bleeps she chickened out and switched off the call. *God how ridiculous, all I'm doing is phoning to say thank you for the flowers.*

Taking a less than ladylike swig of her chardonnay she dialled the number again. After half a dozen or so rings it went to answerphone. A young woman's voice answered:

'Hi, Carlotta and Stuart can't get to the phone right now, but please, don't hang up, leave your name and number and'... Holly banged down the phone. *No, I bloody well won't leave a message! Typical, he doesn't just have a girlfriend, he has a live-in lover...*

She'd ring his mobile. *After all, it would be rude not to acknowledge that beautiful bouquet.* So, psyching herself up, she called, her heart beating furiously.

"Holly, hi, how are you?" He sounded pleased to hear from her. He was obviously out because there was loud music and people talking in animated voices. It was clearly hard for him to hear what she was saying.

"No, no, my pleasure really, it was just a little something to cheer you up," he shouted over the laughing, joking voices. "How's Tess? What?... I can't hear you. Okay, thank you for ringing, can't really talk right now."

Chapter Eleven

The next couple of weeks were the longest Holly could remember. As hard as she tried, she couldn't stop thinking about Stuart and she missed making his waffles in the morning. Janine had gone to visit Ivan in Yorkshire so they couldn't even have their daily chats. And of course, there was no Tess to take out for a walk. Her whole existence revolved around changing sheets, cooking breakfasts and dodging calls from Mac.

Oh well, at least she had Mr Wainwright, who was a very pleasant, appreciative, regular guest. Holly was about to step into the dining room to lay his little table near the window for his breakfast when she saw that the room was flooded. There had been a lot of rain recently, but she never imagined this could happen.

Omg, what am I going to do? I've got guests booked in this week-end.

The whole carpet would have to be ripped up and the floor would have to dry before a new one could be put down. This was a disaster. Holly squelched across the carpet surveying the damage to her tables and chairs. Her feet leaving deep footprints which immediately filled up with water.

She was removing her copper kettles, antique pokers and bellows from the fire place when Mr Wainright poked his head around the door.

"Oh, Mr Wainright, this is a disaster. I never expected this to happen."

"Oh, my dear, what rotten luck. This damn English weather."

"Do you mind having your breakfast in the sitting room?"

"Of course not, my dear."

"I suppose I'd better go and cancel my guests for this

weekend." Holly said dejectedly, during their customary little chat after breakfast, when she collected up his breakfast plates. Mentally counting the cost of her lost earnings.

"No, don't do that dear."

"The dining room is out of action. I don't think I've got much choice."

"A hostess trolley dear, that's what you need."

"A hostess trolley?"

"Yes, marvellous things. My wife had one. Little trolleys that you load up with food, ours even had a hot plate. But your cooked breakfasts will be out, of course, the food will be cold after you've gone up all those stairs, but you could give them a good continental breakfast – you know, with croissants, ham, cheese and the like."

"Mr Wainright. You are a life saver." Holly couldn't stop herself from planting a kiss on his shiny, bald head. "I'll order some right away."

What a godsend that Mr Wainright was staying that week. The hostess trolleys arrived the next day and he spent the next couple of evenings helping Holly assemble them. And he got terribly excited about his proposed menu, suggesting *'corned beef sandwiches and pickled gherkins.'*

O Lord, I'm dreading telling them they can't have a proper cooked breakfast, Holly fretted as her guests trooped in with their various cases. The weather was still awful and they all dripped water into her hall but were very considerate about wiping their feet.

"I'm so sorry, but as you can see we've had some awful weather. My dining room is currently out of action because it got flooded, so would you mind having a continental breakfast instead? I can bring a trolley up and there is a kettle, tea and coffee in your room."

"That's fine, knowing us we'll sleep in and miss breakfast, so that would be perfect," the husband said suggestively. *Um, that's not his wife. Think they've probably got other things rather than breakfast on their mind...*
The other, older couple, were also very gracious.

"We'll be up early anyway, so can wrap something up and take it with us on our walk, thank you dear."
Mr. Wainwright had saved the day.

Chapter Twelve

Oh, if only Stuart were here to help me up with these, Holly thought as she struggled upstairs with the first trolley the next morning. *On second thoughts, he'd probably be highly critical of me daring to give my guests breakfast on these...*

I don't think they are going to want breakfast just now, Holly chuckled as she parked the trolley outside the Gardenia Room. The bed springs were creaking at a fantastic rate. *I hope my old couple are asleep. At least some people are having a nice time.* Holly thought miserably, as she beat a hasty retreat down-stairs for the second trolley. *There isn't going to be any more racing at Goodwood for months now so I probably won't see Stuart again.*

Mail dropped through the letter box as she came downstairs from depositing the second trolley. *Oh lord, there's my bank statement.* Holly didn't have to open it to know that she was severely in the red. The costs of the upkeep on the house were horrendous. *I'm just not pulling enough money in. Stuart is right, most people do want en suite facilities now, they don't want to share bathrooms or toilets. They can do without a fridge, after all I'm not a hotel. Oh, this is all too much. Never mind the weather, I'm going to go out for a ride. I'll speak to the bank manager when I get back.*

The ride did Holly good. Despite the rain, she'd cleared her head and as soon as she walked into the house, she made an appointment to see the bank manager the next day. She'd get a loan and put a bathroom and shower in each room.

She was just cuddling up to Tess on the sofa after collecting her from the vet and was trying to get into watching a little late afternoon TV when the phone rang. To her delight it was Janine.

"Hey Hol, can't talk for long but you need to get yourself glammed up right now. Something sexy and slinky. You've got about an hour, Bye!"

Perplexed, Holly tried to muster up some enthusiasm. *What on earth had her crazy friend in store for her? Please God it isn't some awful blind date.* Holly tried to call back but the phone just went to answer phone. Next thing she knew Janine had sent her a text saying *'Thirty minutes to make yourself irresistible.'*

"S'pose I'd better make an effort, eh Tess?" Can't be a killjoy. Whoever it is, might be nice and at least it will stop me fretting about Stuart and his live-in lover..."

She slipped into her peach, silk Victoria Beckham dress, with its plunging back and elegant scooped neck. A pair of killer heels and a matching pashmina completed her look. Her timing was impeccable. Just as she was making her way down the stairs the doorbell rang and when she opened the door she was staggered to see Stuart.

"Good evening Miss Bradbury," he teased, "Would you do me the honour of escorting me to dinner at the Shard tonight? Your limousine is waiting outside..."

"Stuart! I thought you were in the States..."

She couldn't deny that it was wonderful to see him and had to stop herself from leaping into his arms.

"Change of plan, Miss Bradbury..."

"The Shard? Tonight? But that's in London. Stuart, I can't just leave Willow Cottage, what about Tess? She's just come back from the vet. And my guests, I can't just go off..."

"Yes, you can. It's all sorted, you will be chauffeur-driven back tonight, Janine and Ivan are on their way here now. I took the liberty of arranging a spare key for them with Madge. Dinner is being delivered to them here tonight and Janine said she and Ivan can keep an eye on Tess and your guests. They will even give them breakfast in the morning."

Holly couldn't resist smiling. Lost for words, she took his outstretched hand, and accompanied him out to the chauffeur driven limousine. Two martinis and a dish of olives were at the ready on a little mini-table.

"It's good to see you, how is your arm? We should have gone to A&E, you know. I've been worried about you."

"It's fine. You did a good job, Nurse Bradbury." Holly smiled.

"I never thanked you."

"Thanked me? For what?"

"For tackling that thief and saving the Bugatti... looking after me and Tess."

"Holly, it's okay, you don't need to thank me."

"Yes, I do. Thank you, Stuart. He could have shot you."

"Well, he didn't."

They clinked glasses and shared the olives, both feeling deliciously happy in each other's company.

"Did the police catch the guy?"

"Not that I've heard, sounds like he made a clean get-away."

"Well don't worry, I don't think he will rush back. The whole of Sussex must have heard your alarms."

"That's true." Holly laughed.

Talk then turned to Stuart's up and coming races and before they knew it they had arrived at the Shard.

Holly's breath was taken away by its magnificence. How beautiful it was when it was lit up at night.

She and Mac had always meant to go there for dinner but they never did. In what felt like seconds, a lift whizzed them right up thirty-two floors.

"Oh, my goodness, my stomach flipped, that was so fast," Holly remarked as they stepped out of the lift into the restaurant. It was wonderful, all gleaming glass and polished chrome.

"Mine too," Stuart replied, circling his arm, protectively around her waist. Their table was in prime position right by one of the floor-to-ceiling windows.

"This is fabulous Stuart, thank you."

"My pleasure, Miss Bradbury, Now, let's have some champagne. Here's to celebrating our beautiful Princess Holly escaping the confines of Willow Cottage."

"I will drink to that," Holly smiled, clinking her glass with his. "Sometimes I forget there is a world outside Willow Cottage."

"Yes, I can see that, it seems a strange existence - a young woman in her prime, incarcerated in her castle in the country..."

"I know you don't believe me, but I am happy there..."

"It's a beautiful house Holly, I can understand that, but what took you there? What are you running away from?" He asked, holding her with his eyes.

"Now that would be telling, suffice to say, I wanted a change from living in London town."

"I should tell you about Carlotta..."

Oh no... here goes...

There was a moments awkward silence before Stuart continued.

"She's the young girl who called me *that* night - the one who turned up the next morning... It's not what you think Holly. There is nothing between us. She is like a little sister to me." He took a deep breath.

"She had a twin brother, Benito, who was killed in his first race a couple of months before I came to Goodwood. He was also one of my mechanics and a very good one. When he died, his parents, who are Mexican, were distraught. They struggle financially and relied on Benito to support the family. They were always very good to me and so I didn't hesitate when they asked me to keep an eye on Carlotta. They just couldn't cope with their grief and she needed to get away from the family home. I promised I would look after her. In many ways I blame myself for the death of their son. I was the one who encouraged him out onto the race track."

"That's crazy, Stuart, you weren't to blame."

"I'm not sure Benito's parents see it that way. That's also why I kicked up such a fuss about the press turning up outside your house. I thought they were going to ask questions about Benito. It's all been incredibly painful and I didn't want them hounding Carlotta..."

Holly put her hand over Stuart's.

"Anyway, Carlotta's been staying with me in my apartment in New York since the funeral and she's been following me around like a shadow since she lost her brother. She really likes Chichester and found herself a live-in nannying job with a family just down the road from you in Bosham. That's why she came to see me at Willow Cottage. She had an appointment to meet them later that day and wanted me to go along. The family really took to her, she was great with their kids. She's starting in three months, once she has sorted out her visa. Anyway, now you know. So, tell me, Miss Bradbury how is business?"

"Well, Mr Perone, it could be better ..."

Stuart listened patiently to Holly's financial woes, a crease in his brow.

"Well, it's good that you are making all your rooms en suite but you could be making a lot more money, if you spruced your garden up a bit..."

What's wrong with my garden?

"You could hire the place out for weddings and film shoots."

Um, that might be interesting, I wouldn't mind meeting Tom Hardy.

"Host corporate events?"

Oh no!

"But the place would have to change."

Definitely not.

And so, he went on and on and on. The final straw, being the Bugatti.

"If I was you, I would sell it."

Well, you are not me...

"I bought Willow Cottage because I liked the way it is Stuart. It is quirky and has character. I don't want to rip all that out just to make a few extra quid. I just want to earn enough to manage and go for the odd holiday."

"We're not talking about a few extra quid Holly. Its sink or swim. Doesn't sound to me as if you can carry on much longer the way you are. You say you have problems with the roof and your heating is outdated?"

Holly was sure steam was coming out of her ears.

"And look, your cleaning lady has to go. 'Hair in the bath plug?' And you carry the hoover for her!"

Oh, why did I tell him that?

"And why on earth don't you get the sheets professionally laundered? A company will come and pick them up and deliver them back to you the next morning. That's tax deductible."

I like my sheets and towels to dry in the country air.

"You could then spend that time coming up with a proper business plan. Once you've done that you can see your bank manager..."

Money, money, money... he's as bad as Mac.

"Thank you for your advice Stuart, but I like Willow Cottage the way it is. I don't want it turned into a soul-less corporate enterprise. And whatever you may think, my guests tell me they love staying there. There's the odd exception of course but most of them couldn't care a damn if they don't have a bloody fridge or en suite bathroom. Now if you don't mind I'd like to get back to Willow Cottage tonight. I've got guests to look after, not to mention my dog."

Stuart was the perfect gentleman, he settled the bill and called the Limo but it was only Holly who got in the back.

"Aren't you coming too?"

"No. Jack will drive you to your door."

What was happening? Suddenly, Holly wanted him to jump in the back with her. *Where was he going at this time of night?*

"Drive carefully Jack. Take care, Princess."

And with that he blew her a kiss and walked off into the night. Leaving Holly alone with her frustrated desires.

The house was eerily quiet when Holly crept in. She didn't check the time but it had to be around three o'clock. Janine and Ivan had gone to bed and even Tess didn't stir from the ironing room, where she had a makeshift bed.

Peeking in the kitchen, Holly saw that Janine had done a great job of laying up the hostess trolleys in preparation for breakfast.

I'll sleep in tomorrow. Let Janine take her turn at being a bed and breakfast queen. I don't want to steal her thunder. Oh God, I feel so bloody miserable...

She woke up to the sound of hoovering outside her door. It was nearly lunch time and she had slept in.

"Good morning my lovely, my, you must have needed that lie in?"

"I did, Madge, can't believe I've just woken up, have you had some coffee?"

"Yes, dear, your friends made me some before they went."

Oh no, they've gone. I missed them.

Making her way into the kitchen, Tess tried to jump up from her basket when she saw Holly but was still too weak. Holly gave her a great hug.

"I've missed you, old girl, how are you doing?"

Tess was whining and whimpering madly, over joyed to see her mistress. Holly gave her a chew as she picked up a note from Janine.

Holly darling,

How did you manage lugging up those hostess trollies? Thank God Ivan was here... They all enjoyed their breakfast though so don't worry. Hope you had a great time. Tess has been okay, a bit subdued but she seems to be on the mend, Ivan wants to spend a few days in London at my place before going back to Yorkshire, so we are heading back now. I'm going to be bereft when he goes. Think I'm in love!

Hope you had a fab time. Can't wait to hear all about it.

Love you lots

Janine X

Ps. They are coming to fit your new carpet tomorrow.

x

Dear Janine, I'll have to send her a bouquet of flowers to say thank you. And she's in love, well, no surprise there. Not like her miserable friend who seems to muck up everything with every man she meets...

Holly didn't know what to do with herself. She just couldn't settle to anything.

"Madge," she called up the stairs, "I'm going out for a ride. 'Need to clear my head. If you could lock the front door when you go and leave the key under the flower pot, that would be great. See you tomorrow."

Chapter Thirteen

It was a glorious afternoon. There was nothing like a good canter in the open country-side to take your mind off things. Holly was just turning into the lane leading back to the stables when a tractor came thundering around the corner. Misty started to rear uncontrollably as it was right up close behind her in the narrow country lane.

"Steady girl, steady!"
Holly couldn't control her and was thrown unceremoniously into the bracken at the side of the road while a terrified Misty galloped straight back to the stable.

Appalled at what had happened and with no inkling that it was his fault, the young tractor driver, stopped his tractor and raced over to Holly. Luckily, he had his mobile phone in his pocket.

"Hurry, ambulance please. A lady's been thrown off her horse. She's unconscious. I'm in Appuldram Lane..."

Mr Wainright was perplexed. There was no sign of Holly when he came down for breakfast the next morning. No familiar smell of cooking eggs and bacon. Tess was agitated and whining to be let out the back door and Mr Wainwright's makeshift little table in the sitting room, hadn't been laid for his breakfast.

She must have had a night out on the tiles and slept in, he mused as he let Tess out for a quick run. Oh well, it'll give us something to laugh about later. And gathering up his coat and portfolio of greetings cards he went on his way.

Madge came an hour or so later, 'bissie' at the ready for Tess, who was barking excitedly as Madge rang the doorbell.

Come on Holly dear, where are you? I'm dying to spend a penny...
She was hopping from foot to foot. Still no reply. *Where was she? Tess was going frantic for her bissie. Maybe she'd gone out riding again and left the key under the flower pot. Yes... there it was.*
Letting herself in she made a fuss of Tess and picked up the post from the floor. There was a note from the carpet fitters saying they'd called yesterday afternoon but no one was in. *Strange, Holly was desperate for that carpet to be fitted.*
Taking off her coat and changing her shoes, Madge put on her pinny and got her cleaning box. There were no breakfast plates to clean up and no smells of cooking.
    "Holly? Holly?" Madge called up the stairs.
No reply.
    "Holly, are you there?"
Silence.
Going up the stairs, Madge knocked on her door. No reply. She went inside and saw that her bed was still made. Her handbag was on a chair and so was her coat. Holly never went anywhere without her handbag. Her car was in the drive so she hadn't gone out anywhere. This was all very strange, very unlike Holly.
Madge busied herself flicking a duster, telling herself not to panic, then the doorbell rang and to her horror, a policewoman was standing on the doorstep.
    "Oh, my goodness, has something happened to Holly, is she alright?" Madge was tripping over her words.
    "Are you Miss Bradbury's mother?"
    "No, I'm her cleaning lady."
    "I see, is there a Mr Bradbury?"
    "No, no, there isn't, Holly lives here alone."
    "May I come in a moment?"

Madge felt sick with worry. "Of course, oh please tell me she is alright."

"She is okay, try not to worry. She was thrown off her horse yesterday and has severe concussion. She is in St. Richards and will probably be there for a good week. The owner of the stables called us as her horse went back to the stables without her."

Madge burst into tears. The policewoman put her arm around her, offering to make her a cup of tea, then her walkie-talkie went off and she had to go.

Oh, my goodness, what should I do? Madge was in a major fluster as she knew Holly had guests booked in that night.

Then the phone rang.

Putting on her best voice she picked up the phone.

"Good morning, Willow Cottage, how may I help you?"

"Er, good morning, It's Stuart Perone, Is Holly there?"

"Oh, Mr Perone, I'm so glad it's you… yes, well, no she isn't. I've just heard she is in hospital with a concussion. She had a riding accident yesterday."

"I'll come over. Can you book me a room? I should be with you in two days."

Before Madge could ask him which room he wanted, he'd put down the phone.

Now what? Madge looked in the Bookings book and saw that Holly had another two couples booked in that weekend. Tess started barking again as Mr Wainright came in with his key.

"Oh Mr Wainwright," Madge wailed, I'm so pleased you're here."

"Dear lady, what is it?"

"It's Holly, she's in hospital," Madge sobbed as the whole sorry story came tumbling out.

"Don't worry dear lady. She's a strong young woman, she'll be back soon. In the meantime, we'll just have to manage."

"We?" Madge asked feebly.

"Yes, us dear lady. When the chips are down and all that... now give me that bookings book."

Mr Wainwright and Madge went to visit Holly later that afternoon. She was still quite drowsy but could remember being thrown off Misty.

"That wretched tractor, it was right behind us, scared the living daylights out of Misty. I remember her rearing but nothing after that..."

"You were thrown off into the roadside dear, the tractor driver called an ambulance."

"Right, but Mr Wainwright, what's happening about your breakfast?"

"Don't worry my dear, your dear lady here is sorting me out."

Madge nodded, overcome with pride at her elevated status.

Oh no, I hope she's cooking the sausages properly.

Holly was getting sleepy again, so Mr Wainwright and Madge quietly took their leave.

After leaving the hospital Mr Wainwright and Madge went to the 'Cash'n'Carry' to stock up on provisions. Luckily, Madge knew where Holly kept her trade card.

Well this makes a nice change from spouting on about greetings cards, Mr Wainright mused as they lugged their shopping into the kitchen.

Between them, they prepared the rooms for the two couples who were expected that weekend, and the Johnsons who were arriving that night. Mr Wainwright carrying the hoover and helping Madge with the rigours of the sheets and duvet covers.

"Hospital corners," Madge gently chided him as they tucked in the sheets.

"Oh yes, dear lady, I stand corrected. Hospital corners it is!"

"Now then, dear lady, the Johnsons are due to arrive around six o'clock tonight. I will be here to check them in. Are you alright to get here by eight o'clock tomorrow morning? Keep a note of your extra hours for Holly. Do you want to cook and I'll be the waiter, or shall I cook and you serve the food?"

"Ooh, I'll cook, Madge said rubbing her hands in glee."

"Righto, that's settled then. See you tomorrow morning. Now, I'd better go out and visit a few customers."

The next morning went like clockwork. Mr Wainwright had re-arranged for the carpet fitters to fit the carpet in the dining room after they had served breakfast. Luckily, the guests were not bothered in the least about the bare floor boards and Mr Wainright thoughtfully paid the fitters from his own pocket. Holly could deduct the cost from his bill later.

"Ooh! now that be bootiful," Madge exclaimed, stroking the pile of the very attractive olive- green carpet, "We'd better make sure Tess stays off this. Dog hairs and carpets don't mix."

"Quite right my dear," Mr Wainwright agreed. They made a perfect team. Mr Wainwright made sure he was there to check the guests in. In the short time he had known Holly, she'd told him that at least three people had gone off with her keys...

"Now if we could have payment in advance please, and if you could sign in here with your car registration number, address and telephone number? Oh, and a five pounds, returnable deposit for the keys to your room

and the house, would be capital thank you."
Mr Wainwright then directed them to their rooms and pointed out the 'Bulls Head' and 'The Woolpack' opposite in case they wanted to eat.

"Well then, Tess, that was all tickety-boo. And very nice people they seem too. Only too pleased to pay a deposit for the keys and fill in their car registration numbers."
Then he fixed himself a gin and tonic and got his nose into his greeting cards.

***

"Now you just concentrate on getting better dear," Madge said, giving Holly yet another box of chocolates.

"Thank you so much Madge, you and Mr Wainwright have been marvellous, I can never thank you enough."

"Don't be silly dear, we've been quite a team, I've cooked while Mr Wainwright served the guests."
Oh lord, I hope she didn't give them grease-splattered plates.

"Oh well done, Madge, so what did you cook?"

"Well, the first couple had a full English, three sausages..."
Three? oh heck...

"Two eggs, two rashers of bacon and a hash brown."
Two eggs?

"And the second couple had two boiled eggs each, toast and marmalade."
Oh crikey, soft or hard boiled?

"One had 'ard boiled, the other soft, we found the egg timer, so don't worry dear."

"I'm not worried Madge," Holly fibbed, "I'm sure you and Mr wainwright are doing a splendid job. I don't know what I'd do without you."

Madge felt a warm glow rise to her cheeks, it felt good to be needed and appreciated. But Holly was tiring so she quietly picked up her bag to leave.

"Oh Madge," she just managed, before closing her eyes, "Don't forget to check for snail trails."

"I won't dear, first thing I do when I go into the dining room."

"Thank you, Madge, you are a star."

"Oh, Holly dear, I forget to tell you that your Mr Perone is coming over, very upset he was when I told him what's happened."

But Holly was nodding off and clearly hadn't registered what Madge said about Stuart's imminent visit.

***

"Now these are delicious scones," Mr Wainwright remarked, as he took another dollop of strawberry jam.

"Well, one thing I can do is bake," Madge remarked, "Been doing it since I was a child. My Eddie loved my scones." Madge said sadly.

"I can see why," said Mr Wainright, "May I?" he asked, taking another one.

"Oh yes, please do, Mr Wainwright, they are best the day you make them. There's nothing like a good old English tea, my Eddie used to say."

Mr Wainwright had a light-bulb moment.

"Cream teas! That's it! Holly could make a fortune. A few nice tables and chairs in her back garden, this is the perfect spot for passing trade."

"Oh now, Mr Wainwright, that be a very good idea That would help her pay a few bills".

"It certainly would dear lady."

Stuart arrived in London the next afternoon. Hailing a cab, he went straight to visit Holly in hospital from the airport. She was asleep when he got there.

She looked so young and fragile. Her face devoid of make-up and her beautiful thick hair fanning out around her pillow. Gently taking her hand, he kissed her fingers.

"Shh, Princess," he said stroking her cheek. "I've come all the way to England to see my beautiful little 'B&B Queen' only to find her in a hospital bed."

"Stuart, what are you doing here?" Holly smiled, trying to sit up.

"Hey now, be careful," he said protectively, fiddling with the controls to raise the bed head. "Well your heart rate has gone up since I came into the room. So, I'll take that as a good sign," he joked, as he studied one of the machines she was hooked up to.

"You will be back home before you know it. Everything is under control at Willow Cottage, Oliver and Madge are quite a team."

"Now, don't you go bossing them about," Holly teased.

"I wouldn't dare. They are diamonds. They love you Miss Bradbury. But then everybody does..."

"I don't know about that."

"Well, I do". He said fixing her with his eyes.

They were silent for a moment as neither knew what to say.

"So, how are you feeling? Do you remember much about the accident?"

"Bits... I remember the horse rearing and being thrown off. Not much after that... I'm okay but get tired quickly.

"Well, I know how you like your perfume so I bought you some on the plane."

"Oh Stuart, thank you that's so sweet." *Chanel no. 5, what a great choice."*

"You know you look really sweet without your make-up."

"Oh, thanks for reminding me, I'm not wearing any!"

"You don't need it Miss Bradbury, you are beautiful just as you are."

"So, you don't like my make-up?"

"I didn't say that... yes I do, you just look younger and innocent without it. But of course, we both know you aren't as innocent as you look..."

"The same could be said about you Mr Perone."

A kindly nurse cut short their banter by reminding Stuart that the patients were about to be served dinner and visiting would resume in the evening.
Kissing Holly on the cheek, Stuart told her to tuck in to her meal, and promised to be back soon.

Mr Wainwright, opened the door to him as he was in the dining room sorting through his customers' orders for greetings cards.

"Now young sir," Mr Wainright swung into B&B mode. "I'm sure we can offer you a room. If you could please sign in the guest book, with your car registration and contact details? Then, if you would like a key to the house - it's a five pounds returnable deposit."
Stuart produced a nice crisp five-pound note and duly signed in the book.

"Looks like you are doing a fine job here, Mr Wainright. This signing-in book and deposit for the keys is a great idea, so much more secure for Holly. I'm Stuart by the way," he said shaking hands.

"Ah yes... of course, you are the racing driver... I've seen you at breakfast. Oliver Wainright, very pleased to make your fine acquaintance. Now. I think our Holly needs a little help at the moment."

"She certainly does," Stuart agreed. "I've just been to see her and it sounds to me as if you and Madge have been doing a great job of holding things together.

Do her parents know that she is in hospital?"

"Yes, they do, but are currently away at their villa in Spain. Madge and I assured them that things are okay here, so there was no need for them to rush back. Holly said she speaks to them on the phone every day from hospital."

"That's good." said Stuart.

"Mr Perone! It's you!" Madge came rushing out of the kitchen, her hands covered in flour. "Would you like to try one of my cream teas?"

"I'd love to, thank you." Minutes later he was savouring her wonderful scones and home-made strawberry jam.

"Um Madge... these are excellent."

"Glad you think so," Mr Wainwright cut in enthusiastically "Because we think Holly could do a nice little trade in cream teas."
Madge was grinning from ear to ear.

"Now, that is a great idea," Stuart agreed. "Could you keep up with the baking Madge?"

"Oh yes, Mr Perone, I've been baking since I was a little girl. Its second nature to me."

"I think you should both go and put your excellent idea to Holly. If she goes for it, I can erect a sign outside the house. Get a few tables and chairs for the garden..."

"Ooh, now that would be bootiful," exclaimed Madge, "Shall we go then Mr Wainright? visiting starts again in half an hour."
Stuart smiled as he watched them go off.

A couple of hours later they were back. Madge was beaming from ear to ear.

"She wants me to start baking tomorrow, try my first batch out on the guests, with a complimentary afternoon, cream tea."

Chapter Fourteen

Stuart was looking around the garden. He estimated there would be enough space for eight little tables and chairs, complete with sun shades. There was access to a ground floor toilet through the rear entrance of the house facing the back garden where Stuart and Mr Wainwright would set up the tables and chairs. Holly had an up to date hygiene certificate so all he had to do was erect a sign inviting passing trade to turn into the garden. There was even parking space to comfortably fit half a dozen or so cars.

He commissioned a local sign maker to create an attractive sign advertising '*Willow Cottage' Cream Teas, in the tranquility of an English Country Garden,*' which would be erected at the front of the house. At five pounds a head for a nice pot of English tea, two of Madge's delicious scones, home-made jam and cream, Holly should make a nice little extra earner. Of course, Madge was in her element and clapped her little pudgy hands with glee when she saw the stylish, Italian garden furniture in the garden. Mr Wainwright was over the moon with the Cream Tea sign and had insisted on erecting it himself in the front garden.

Holly was coming home the next day and as Stuart would hopefully, be busy serving cream teas, Mr Wainwright said he and Madge would collect her from hospital.

"Well, she will either love or loathe this venture, Tess," he said scratching the dog fondly behind her ears. "Let's hope she loves it, eh?"
Stuart liked to think that Tess's doe eyes were rooting for him.

Around four o'clock the next day, Mr Wainwrights' car tootled down the drive. Stuart was in the throes of serving a cream tea to a charming American couple, who were enthralled by the stream at the bottom of the garden. The birds were tweeting happily and the Hollyhocks and Delphiniums were gently swaying in a light, perfumed breeze. It was a beautiful afternoon, with a bee busily humming in a big clump of sweet-smelling lavender.

Just as he walked back into the house with his empty tray he came face to face with Holly.

"Stuart?"

"Holly…"

"You look busy…"

"Yes, Holly dear," Mr Wainright cut in, "Come into the sitting room and sample one of Madge's scones."

"Oh, okay, thank you."

Stuart meanwhile had dashed back into the kitchen and was plating up another couple of cream teas for some new customers in the garden. *Let's hope she approves of our efforts… right then, some of Madge's wonderful home-made strawberry jam, one generous dollop of cream, and we are in business…*

"Holly dear, did you notice the sign for cream teas as we came down the drive?" Mr Wainwright asked cautiously.

"No, I didn't, wow, these are delicious Madge."

"Do you remember our discussing the idea of offering your guests a cream tea? Well, while you have been recuperating this last week, Madge here, has been putting her baking skills to good use and we are starting to attract some passing trade… In fact, dear, we've put together a little café in your garden…"

"Oh wow, that's wonderful."

"You think so?"

"Of course? Why wouldn't I? And you've got Stuart waitressing?" Holly laughed, "I bet this was his idea?"

Well actually, no, it wasn't dear. It was mine."

***

"So, you don't mind about the cream teas?" Stuart asked Holly as they enjoyed a gin and tonic in the garden later that evening. "I thought you might have thought we were getting a bit above ourselves?"

"I think it's a great idea. Thank you, Stuart, for all your efforts. You quite suit wearing a pinny..."

"Yes, well, I'm more comfortable wearing my racing gear," Stuart smiled. "So how are you feeling?"

"A bit woozy, but I will be okay. It's wonderful to see you."

"It's great to see you too," Stuart said, putting his hand over hers and gently lifting her fingers to his lips.

"You've got more bookings coming up and Madge and Mr Wainright have everything in hand."

"I know, I don't know what I would have done without them. Or you."

"I think they are enjoying working together." Stuart said, winking.

"Ooh good! Romance at Willow Cottage?"

"Yes, romance at Willow Cottage," Stuart smiled, causing Holly to blush from head to toe.

"Look Holly, I'm racing in Monaco next week and I'd like you to come with me. It would only be for a couple of days."

Holly's heart leapt into her mouth.

"I'd love to..."

Chapter Fifteen

"Now are you sure you will be okay Mr Wainright? This is my number and my parents are back from Spain now so you can always contact them."

"We will be fine dear, now off you go and have a good time."

"Now that Madge is cooking and baking, I've arranged for Abigail, a girl from the village to come in, do the cleaning and waitressing. Her brother, Tom, will also take Tess out for a short walk every day."

"Capital, now off you go!"

"Thank you, Oliver," Stuart warmly shook Mr Wainwright's hand then kissed Madge on the cheek before they drove off to the airport.
Tess was looking sadly through the window in the sitting room. Ears down.

"Ooh just one moment," Holly whispered, rushing back in the house.

"Good bye darling," she said burying her face in Tess' sturdy neck. "Look after everyone. I will be back soon."

Nestled on the coast of the French Riviera, the principality of Monaco was a hive of activity in anticipation of Formula One's most famous race. The Monaco Grand Prix. The rich and famous were arriving in droves, in private planes and luxury yachts and boats. Holly had never seen so many "beautiful people" in one place. This was undeniably the 'Glamorous set' as her mother would say.

The staff at their hotel clearly knew Stuart and went out of their way to make them feel welcome. That evening they dined on the terrace overlooking the bay of Monaco. Although excited about the race, Holly couldn't help feeling anxious. Reading her mind, Stuart tried to reassure her.

"It's what I do Hol. Yes, it's dangerous, but that is the thrill."

They spent the most wonderful night together. Now Holly knew what it was like to really desire a man. He was still sleeping and the sun was filtering through the window into their room. Holly just wanted to hold him close. To keep him with her in the safety of this room, forever. *What if these are the last moments we ever have together? Supposing he crashes? Suffers some terrible injury or worse?*

Stuart stirred, traced her lips with his finger and kissed her.

"Good morning beautiful."

Holly held him in her gaze.

"I'll be okay Holly, my Saint Christopher keeps me safe, I never race without it."

"I know, now kiss me again..."

After a light breakfast on the terrace, they made their way to the race track. Walking into the Pit, she saw Stuart's red and white Ferrari. A team of mechanics were already working on it, checking the engine and tyres. There was a highly charged atmosphere of anticipation and excitement with the roaring of the engines, smell of petrol and clusters of eager young and older, seasoned mechanics, each protecting and nurturing their own particular 'baby.' Holly spotted a couple of famous drivers who shook hands and patted Stuart on the back. This was a den of roaring testosterone.

"Come with me," Stuart said taking Holly by the hand and leading her into a side room. "This looks about your size, he said, holding up a white, Formula One leather racing suit and helmet. You can slip it on in here."

"OMG Stuart, I'm going in your car?"

"Not mine, that's a single seater. I've borrowed one of the Marshall's cars so we can go for a quick warm up around the practice lap.

As Holly climbed in, the mechanics helped her with her seat belt and checked her helmet. Then, patting her convivially on the helmet and giving her the thumbs up, they smiled her on her way.

Stuart was revving the engine. The car was shuddering like an angry cat. Seconds later they blasted off like a rocket. Holly's stomach was in her mouth, they were going so fast. Luckily, the roaring of the engine and screeching of the tyres drowned her screaming.

She was petrified but ecstatic at the same time. It made going on a roller coaster feel like a ride on a toddler's roundabout. But before she knew it they had completed the lap and were driving back into the pit. Stuart took off his helmet and shook out his mane of dark, shiny hair.

"So how was that?"

Holly could hardly speak. Taking off her helmet she took a long, deep breath. Her legs felt like jelly.

"Now I know what a near death experience feels like," she smiled... "It was fantastic, I loved it." She said, throwing her arms around him.

"Good, we will do it again."

Oh lord, not too soon please.

"I have to go now Holly. Juan's wife, Isabella, will take you where you can watch the race and cheer me on with champagne..."

Holly felt sick with nerves... *Oh, for god sake stop it, don't let him see you like this.*

"I will be fine, I have my Saint Christopher, now go and cheer for me. I have a race to win."

Before they could even kiss, Isabella was at her side.

After a quick introduction, Isabella linked Holly's arm and led her away to a waiting car.
Turning around Holly blew him a kiss.
Be safe my darling.

It was going to be a dangerous race. Ambulance and safety cars were strategically parked all along the circuit built around the narrow streets of Monaco. The drivers would have to use all their precision and skill to race through the tight corners.
Just the year before, two had crashed and ended up in the harbour. Stuart told Holly that "Winning the Monaco Grand Prix was worth two races anywhere else in the world." And of course, he was desperate to win.
Spectators were crowding in the temporary grandstands built all around the circuit and the harbour. Millionaires and no doubt, billionaires, were regularly arriving in their boats and yachts as people watched from their balconies. This was an event when many residents and hotels cashed in on their bird's eye view of the arrival of these celebrities as much as the race itself.
Holly was with the wives and families of the drivers in the sumptuous Ermanno Palace Penthouse, famous for the best view of the race.
"Is this the first time you have watched Stuart race?" Isabella asked.
"Yes, it is," Holly answered. "To be honest I will be pleased when it is over."
"I know, I feel the same. My heart is in my mouth the whole time. I actually feel sick when I see Juan get in the car. I am sorry to say that it doesn't get any easier."
The champagne was flowing and Holly sipped her drink thoughtfully.
Well, I will just have to get used to it… He will be okay, he

has his Saint Christopher. He may even win.

The atmosphere was tense as wives and family members were glued to the race, either watching through the windows with their vast panoramic view of the race or on huge, specially erected plasma screens. Stuart was doing well and was currently in fifth place with Juan hot on his heels.

"Oh no, now they are approaching the tunnel," Isabella made the sign of the cross and uttered a prayer in Spanish.

"Isabella, what's the matter?"

"The tunnel is really dangerous. They have to adjust their vision when they go in as its dark then, when they come out, its suddenly light again and they're in the fastest point of the track."

Oh Lord, why did she tell me that, Please, please let him be okay. It doesn't matter if he wins or not, just keep him safe…

Holly held her breath until she saw Stuart emerge from the tunnel, he then had to brake suddenly in order to negotiate the famous hairpin bend.

Phew, he's done it! Thank goodness.

But then one of the tyres exploded on the car just in front of Stuart, causing it to veer across the track and crash into the barrier. The driver's wife shrieked and ran from the room. There was a horrible hush as all the other wives felt secretly relieved that its wasn't their loved-one who had crashed. Race Marshalls scrambled onto the track waving red flags as the race was temporarily halted. Miraculously, it wasn't a serious crash, the driver was okay and the track was cleared in minutes.

The crowds applauded as the race resumed and two laps later, Holly's heart was in her mouth as she watched Stuart roar into fourth place. People were waving flags and cheering the drivers on as the race was drawing to a close. After having fallen back into fifth place, Stuart miraculously came in third. Holly was ecstatic.

The press was having a field day, TV cameras and journalists were everywhere, recording the day's exhilarating events. Prince Albert of Monaco and his glamorous wife, Princess Charlene, were standing near the rostrum to present Stuart and the two drivers who won first and second place with their trophies. Following the special tradition of the Monaco Grand Prix the winners left their cars on the track and walked to the royal box. Tears ran down Holly's cheeks as Stuart stepped up to the podium. The national anthem of each winner rang out to the crowd as they were presented with their trophies. Stuart kissed and held his coveted trophy above his handsome head as his team mates sprayed magnums of champagne. It was a spectacular day. Holly practically jumped into his arms after the ceremony.

"Congratulations Stuart, you were magnificent." She said hugging him and savouring the smell of his skin.

"Thank you, Princess, I'm glad you escaped your castle. It's wonderful to have you here."

"Really?"

"Yes, really," he said holding her with his eyes. "Come on," he said, taking her by her hand, "Let's get back to our hotel. We've been invited to about three parties tonight on the various yachts around the harbour. And I need to get out of this suit." He said, winking.

People were cheering and patting him on the back as they walked back to their hotel. Journalists and photographers jostled each other, all eager for pictures and quotes.

"So how does it feel Stuart, to come third?" one called out.

"Fantastic, I'm really happy."

"Do you feel confident you can win the Abu Dhabi Grand Prix?"

"Yes of course, so long as I have my lucky mascot by my side," Stuart joked, indicating Holly.

"Where are you off to now?"

"Prince Ali Razia's yacht for a party - after I've freshened up of course!"

As soon as they reached their hotel room Stuart put the '*Do not disturb sign*' on their door. The champagne was on ice and ready in their room. Popping the cork, they sank into the bubbles of the Jacuzzi in their bathroom and relived the excitement of the day before exploring the delights of each other's bodies in that huge, sumptuous bed.

"Come on Princess, we need to show our faces at the party."

Holly groaned.

"I know, I wish we could stay here too," he said kissing her neck.

Holly slipped into her scarlet, figure-hugging ankle length dress with its plunging back, then stepped into her black Christian Louboutin shoes.

"Um, my scarlet lady," Stuart teased approvingly. "Let's go before I ravage you again!" Taking her hand, they stepped into the lift to the ground floor. The streets of Monaco were packed with the glitterati. You could almost smell the sense of celebration in the air.

An hour or so later, they boarded Prince Ali Razia's super-yacht. The party was in full swing with photographers and on-lookers on the marina snapping pictures of the party goers.

Music was booming from the lower deck where people were dancing. The middle deck was quieter, with people chatting, sipping champagne and cocktails while being served the most magnificent canapes by waitresses who looked like models; their enviably long, shapely, brown legs shown off to perfection in their nautical shorts, shirts and captain's caps. All the racing drivers were there alongside former racing legends and their partners.

The upper deck was beautifully peaceful. This was the place to go for lovers. Savouring the twinkling lights and majesty of the surrounding bay of Monaco as the boat bobbed peacefully on the water. Everywhere Holly looked there were famous faces and Prince Ali Razia was the perfect host, insisting that they stay the night in one of his luxury cabins.

It was a magical night. But the most wonderful thing was knowing that they only had eyes for each other.

After a delicious champagne breakfast on the upper deck the next morning, Prince Ali Razia invited Stuart and Holly for a quick helicopter ride around the main sights of Monaco. Holly caught her breath as they flew over the beautiful, sprawling, "Palais Princier," from which the Grimaldi family has ruled since the thirteenth century.

"Ooh look, there's the rock of Monaco and the cathedral where Prince Albert got married," Holly said excitedly.

"It's also where Prince Rainier and Princess Grace are buried. Now, she was a real princess," he teased, stroking Holly's neck.

A quick turn and they were flying over the Formula One Grand Prix racing circuit and opulent Monte Carlo Casino.

"That's where we are going tonight," Stuart said, squeezing Holly's hand. "You're going to be my lucky mascot," he said kissing her cheek.

Willow Cottage and Holly's nightly ritual of laying her tables for breakfast the next morning felt a world away as she stepped into the exquisite Monte Carlo casino on Stuart's arm later that night. Ferraris, Bentleys and Rolls Royce's were parked around the front of the casino. All had personalised number plates. Uniformed Valets were zipping in and out of them as their owners sauntered into the casino.

The palatial decor exuded a mood full of romance, the presence of Royalty, the rich and famous. It was like stepping into a film set.

Stuart was Holly's James Bond.

Chapter Sixteen

Madge and Mr Wainwright had done a sterling job of holding everything together at Willow Cottage. The cream teas had taken off a treat, with a regular summer-time passing trade and optional extra for Holly's 'B&B' guests.

Abigail, was a wizard at cleaning, allowing Madge to concentrate on baking and cooking the breakfasts. *So, Willow Cottage can survive without me. Maybe I will go away more often!* Holly mused. But her beloved Tess had pined for her and Holly was over the moon at seeing her gentle giant again.

Life slowly returned to normality for Holly at Willow Cottage. Guests came and went. Madge and Mr Wainwright, she noticed, were becoming increasingly comfortable in each other's company. Holly and Janine still enjoyed their morning chats and Holly was over-joyed when Janine told her she had been promoted to senior staff writer at '*Smile.*' She and Ivan were still an item, spending alternate weekends together in Yorkshire and London.

But there was a huge hole in Holly's heart for Stuart. After their wonderful time in Monaco he had to fly straight back to the States and then he was off to race in Bahrain. Six whole weeks until she saw him again and then what? He was based in New York and she was in Chichester...

Chapter Seventeen

One Year later

Stuart had a great year. He'd won the Spanish Grand Prix and come second in the Driver's Championship. He and Holly spoke on the phone practically every day and he came over to Willow Cottage as often as he could between racing all over the world.

Holly's lovely Madge and dear Mr Wainright had got married and were moving to Dorset as Mr Wainwright was retiring from his job selling greetings cards. Madge's mother was moving with them but going into residential care nearby. Holly couldn't have been happier for them, and she and Stuart were chief witnesses at their wedding in Chichester. The reception of course, was held at Willow Cottage.

All the bedrooms at Willow Cottage were now en suite and Holly was making a 'pretty penny' with regular guests staying during the famous Goodwood racing season. Madge had found a delightful local lady to take on the task of baking for the cream teas because one thing Holly just couldn't get her head around was baking.

Then Holly realised she was late for her period. She and Stuart discussed having a baby and Stuart said he would be "over the moon" if she became pregnant. But Holly was so busy running Willow Cottage she didn't give it much thought, preferring to think that 'What will be, will be.' Besides, Stuart was still busy with his racing career.

But two weeks ran into three weeks. Holly and Janine still had their morning chats and Holly finally confided her worries to her friend.

"I'm scared Janine, what if I am pregnant and he isn't happy?"

"Oh, come on Hol, you've discussed this and he said he would be fine. You need to find out."

"Yes, you are right."

"Well, I think it is really exciting! I might even learn to knit!"

So, Holly bought a pregnancy testing kit. Taking a deep breath, she forced herself to do the test. As she thought, the line turned blue. It was positive.

She quickly got on the phone to Janine.

"Janine! its blue!"

"What?"

"The lines turned blue. Its positive. I'm pregnant."

"Congratulations. That's fantastic. Margery? Everyone? Holly is pregnant!"

There was a resounding cheer in the office. But Holly didn't dare be happy until she told Stuart.

"Should I tell him on the phone or face to face?"

"Well, if it was me I'd tell him now."

"Yes, but I need to see his face, to tell what his reaction is."

"Holly, he isn't Mac."

But Stuart wasn't coming to the UK for another two weeks.

Oh Lord, I've told Janine and now everyone on the magazine knows, I will tell him tonight.

But she didn't.

I must see his face...

***

At last Stuart was coming back to Willow Cottage. Holly had booked a nice little French restaurant for lunch in Chichester. It was one of their favourites. He loved the food there.

Here goes, now or never.

"Stu, I have some news."

"Yes?"

Holly's eyes were firmly fixed on the table cloth. Images of Mac and that terrible night in the restaurant in London flashed into her mind.

"C'mon, it can't be that bad," Stuart said taking her hand.

"Well no, I'm hoping it's good."

He was looking at her expectantly in between dipping some ciabatta into a particularly delicious garlic and oil dip.

"I'm pregnant."

"Oh darling, that is fantastic news. I am going to be a father... wow, it feels good, really good," he said, raising her hand to his lips.

"Are you sure? You really are happy?"

"Of course, I'm sure, why wouldn't I be?"

His eyes said it all. He was happy. Joyously happy. And so was Holly.

Holly called her parents when they got back to Willow Cottage.

"Hello, Worpleston 2149"

Holly smiled. Her mother had always answered their house phone, with an announcement of the phone number. Auntie Maud had done the same.

After an initial chat about Holly's 'B&B' escapades, how miserable the weather was in England and how Dad wanted to sell their house and move lock, stock and barrel to Spain, Holly broke her happy news.

"Oh, my goodness, darling, I'm going to be a grandmother! About time too. I thought it would never happen..."
"Oh, thanks…"
"I'll get my knitting needles out."
Oh no, can't you just pop into Gap instead? Holly's mum was famous in the family for her unorthodox knitting. Somehow everything she made was two sizes too big and never resembled the pattern.
"That would be lovely mum, thank you."
"We haven't even met Stuart yet dear? Are we likely to, with all his gadding about?"
"I have suggested it lots of times, Mum, but you and Dad are always in Spain. We'll fix something up, he really wants to meet you both.
"Well, make sure you do and keep me posted about that bump of yours. Make sure you eat liver at least once a week. It's full of iron. You'll need it changing all those sheets. I'll call you when we get to Spain. Should be sometime after seven tonight. Cheerio and congratulations dear. Dad will be over the moon…"

Holly knew that once her mother was in her sunshine paradise she'd forget to call, besides, Stuart had booked a surprise visit to Paris that night. She didn't have any guests booked in and Abigail and her brother were going look after Tess.

Four hours later they were in Paris.
"Oh, Stu this is lovely," Holly exclaimed as they checked in to the typically French, family run hotel just off the main square in Montmartre.
They had to suppress a smile as a rather arrogant looking young boy had just been nipped by a lobster he'd taken out from a tank in the foyer to show his friends. The Madame on the reception desk, with a face

like thunder, was in the middle of telling him to put it back when Holly and Stuart walked in with their bags. Rolling her eyes, she explained in broken English that her son was trying to impress his friends.

"Poor thing will probably end up on our table tonight," Stuart joked.

"Oh, don't Stuart I can't bear to think of it being boiled."

After a brief rest they made their way to the metro.

"Oh wow, Stu, the Eifel Tower! Holly exclaimed.

"Yes, and we're going to climb to the top."

"What?"

"No, we'll take the elevator." Stuart smiled as he kissed her cheek, "Do you think I'd let my pregnant lady walk up those steps?"

"I wouldn't put anything past you," Holly grinned as they waited for the lift.
The tower was beautiful and lit up with thousands of tiny lights. Looking closely, they could see inscriptions of the names of all the people who had helped build it back in 1887. Holly snuggled into Stuart as they went higher. As luck would have it, they were the only people right at the top.

"Wow, what a view," Holly remarked. Oh look, there's the Sacré-Coeur..."

"Holly, there is something I need tell you. Something you don't know about me."
Oh no, what?

"I am an old-fashioned kind of guy. You have tamed me Princess, and I want to free you from that castle of yours. Will you marry me?"

"My goodness Stuart," Holly's eyes filled with tears, "Yes, yes I will."
Fishing in his jacket pocket he pulled out a little black velvet box.

"Go on open it."

It was a single solitaire diamond.

"Oh Stu, its beautiful. Thank you."

"Does it fit?"

"Yes, it's perfect, Holly laughed showing it off."

"Good," he laughed, "Now let's go and get something to eat. I'm starving."

They decided to go to back to Montmartre, Paris' famous artists' quarter. As they sipped their Kir Royales in a bustling cafe, at least three street artists, eager for a sale, started to sketch a picture of them. Without thinking twice Holly, bought one. *This will always be a very special picture. I'll find somewhere to hang it in Willow Cottage.*

Her thoughts turned to the picture of Miss Gibbons and the children. It was impossible to tell if any of them were happy. Not so with this picture. There was no doubting how happy she and Stuart were at that moment.

Adoration emanated from Stuart's eyes as he watched her admiring the picture. *Now was a good time.*

"I'm going to give up racing Holly."

"Why?"

"I'm going to be a husband and a father. It's just too risky…"

"But Stu, racing is your life."

"Not anymore," he said taking her hand in his across the table.

"I don't want to clip your wings Stu."

"You haven't… How would you feel about selling Willow Cottage and moving to the States? I've been approached by one of the TV sports networks to present their motor racing channel. I've still got my modelling contract for Gaff trainers, but long term, I think presenting is the answer."

Holly's stomach did a loop. *Sell Willow Cottage? Her forever home.*

"We can take Tess with us."

Holly knew that a man like Stuart would never be content running a 'B&B'. Her heart told her she had to follow him.

"Okay, let's move to the States. And yes, Tess is coming with us!"

Chapter Eighteen

Stuart wanted to get married as soon as possible. On their return from Paris they went into the Registry Office in Chichester and booked their wedding. They also went into the estate agent Holly bought Willow Cottage through, and made an appointment with one of the agents for the house to be valued and put on the market.

When Stuart and Holly's special day came, Holly's Dad drove Holly to the registry office in the Bugatti which he'd festooned with white ribbons. Holly looked resplendent in a lovely long, off-the-shoulder, ivory silk dress that showed her seven-month bump off to perfection. Her hair was up in a 'Billy Holiday' jazz singer, type style, specially pinned with a beautiful ivory coloured Gardenia.

"You look gorgeous darling," her father said, giving her a kiss just after he helped her out of the car.

"Are you happy?"

"Yes, Dad, more than I ever imagined…"

"That's good, very good," he said, a tear in his eye. "Right then, we've got a wedding to go to…"

Madge and Mr Wainwright were sitting at the front of the Registry office, next to Holly's Mum, Stuart's Mother and Carlotta. Ivan and Janine were witnesses. Margery and other colleagues and friends from Holly's journalism days were also there, as were Stuart's racing pals.

"You look beautiful," Stuart whispered in her ear just before they took their vows.

"And you look fab," Holly whispered.

He did indeed look wonderful in a charcoal grey designer suit, a simple white rose bud, pinned in his lapel. Holly thought her heart would burst with happiness as he said "I do," and slipped the wedding ring on to her finger.

As they walked down the aisle and out into the Chichester sunshine, friends and family cheered and clapped while Janine, Margery and Holly's Mum showered a beaming 'Mr and Mrs Perone' with a special confetti of fragrant lavender and rose petals. Cameras clicked as passers-by stopped to admire the glamorous couple posing for the cameras. Holly's Dad then made an announcement:

"Everybody, can I please have your attention for a moment? Can you all please follow me, in your cars. All will be revealed when we arrive…"

"Oh goodness, what's he up to?" Holly looked at Stuart. "I don't remember this being in the plan."

Stuart feigned ignorance as Holly's Dad drove them in the Bugatti to the Goodwood race course, followed by all the wedding party in their cars. They'd secretly arranged for Stuart to complete a lap of honour around the track with his new wife. Everyone cheered and honked their car horns and Holly's Dad sprayed a magnum of champagne, being careful not to shower the bride and groom after they'd completed their lap in the wonderful, league of its own, Bugatti.

The reception of course, was at Willow Cottage, which had been beautifully decorated with silver tasselled designer balloons, organised by Margery and Janine. Simple displays of white, country cottage style flowers were on every table and a fantastic arrangement of huge white ostrich feathers dominated the dining room.

Champagne and delicious food followed in abundance, served by Holly's beloved Madge and Mr Wainwright, who both insisted on helping at the reception. Madge had even kindly made their wedding cake. Three chocolate and ginger heart-shaped cakes in a lovely traditional wedding tier. One for Holly, one for Stuart and one for their baby.

"The cake is gorgeous Madge, thank you so much." Holly hugged her. "And thank you both for everything," she said, feeling emotional. I don't know what I would have done without you. You are wonderful friends."

"Well, if it wasn't for you, we wouldn't have met," Madge said, looking adoringly at Mr Wainwright.

"That's right, and we love working together, don't we dear? Think we've got the bug after serving all those cream teas!"

"Well, don't you two forget to eat something," Holly said, giving them both a plate.

"Holly, you look beautiful." Janine kissed her friend on the cheek. "You've got that pregnancy glow."

"Well, I never thought I'd be wearing such a large sized wedding dress," Holly laughed."

"Can't wait to kick off these heels though. Think my days of killer heels are over – for the next couple of months at least."

"Guess what?" Janine whispered, I'm not just a bride's maid this time…"

"Ooh Janine, you mean…?"

"Yes, Ivan and I are going to get married. There must be something about this house. First, it's Madge and Mr Wainright, then you and Stuart and now Ivan and me. He proposed as you and Stuart were driving around the track."

"I'm so happy for you," Holly hugged her friend. You'll be a fabulous '*Mr and Mrs*.' What are your plans?"

"Well, just call me 'Mrs James Herriot,' I'm going to help Ivan run his practice in Yorkshire and maybe do a little freelance writing on the side... So, who are you going to give your bouquet to now?"

Holly knew exactly.

Mr Wainwright then tapped his champagne glass.

"Ladies and Gentlemen, please be upstanding for the Father of the bride."

The room quietened.

After some emotional words about how special his daughter was and a few funny jokes about Holly growing up, Holly's Dad concluded his tribute:

"Well Holly darling, what can I say? You have been a joy to have as a daughter and I know you will be a wonderful wife and mother. Everything you do you do with passion. First it was your journalism, then it was running Willow Cottage. You are now going on to pastures new with a wonderful young man who, I thank the lord, appreciates a fine motor car. Mary and I are delighted to welcome him into our family Everyone please raise your glass to Stuart and Holly."

"To Stuart and Holly." Everyone responded.

Stuart then stood up to say a few words.

"Basil and Mary, I thank you for your daughter, my beautiful wife. She captured my heart the first day she made my breakfast as a guest here at Willow Cottage. Even though she had to practise boiling my eggs, wasn't happy that I have a 'thing' about ice and prefer waffles to toast, something drew us together and I can truly say that I am the happiest man. So, I'm not going to 'waffle' on, and would just like to make a 'toast' of another sort. To my beautiful wife, my Princess, my 'B&B queen'."

Everyone applauded while Holly suppressed a tear.

Holly's Mum then jumped up and related a few touching words of her own. It was a wonderful day, everybody danced until dawn and Holly and Stuart couldn't have wished for a more perfect wedding.

***

On their first day as Mr and Mrs Stuart Perone, with 'Bump on Board,' they drove down to the pretty little cemetery in Eastbourne where Aunt Maud was buried. Standing proudly in front of the grave with Stuart, Holly placed her wedding bouquet near the battered old picture of Auntie Maud's sweetheart, Colin. Just at that moment, a lovely, little white feather dropped at Holly's feet. Auntie Maud had always been her guardian angel.

Holly just knew that it was from her.

Chapter Nineteen

Five months later

"Good morning, I'm Milly Henderson, I've come for the viewing?"

"Yes, of course, I'm Holly Perone, come in. This is Tess, her bark is a lot worse than her bite, don't worry." Milly was worried and kept a wide berth.

"Your baby is lovely, how old is he?... She?"

"She. Ivy, three months." Holly answered proudly, jiggling her on her hip.

Milly immediately fell in love with the house. Holly had kept the tapestries and pictures of various country scenes adorning the walls of the entrance hall. The Baxters had no use for them and gladly let her have them. Same with the small table by the front-door, which was still crowded with business cards and tourist guides of every shape and size.

Following Holly, baby and dog, Milly made her way past a large kitchen and laundry room into a spacious back sitting room with a very attractive, open brick fireplace.

A large framed photograph of a very handsome young man, in a Formula One racing suit, spraying a magnum of champagne hung above the fireplace.

"That's Ivy's Dad, he'd just won a major race at Goodwood. He was one of my first guests and we ended up getting married." Holly said proudly.

"Oh, my goodness, how lovely," said Milly.

There was also a beautiful wedding photograph of the two of them proudly displayed on top of a baby grand piano in the corner of the room.

"Yes, Willow Cottage was a very lucky move for me."

"It was?" Milly asked hopefully, "Oh sorry dear, I didn't mean to pry."

Holly could sense that this lovely lady was facing some cross-roads in her life. Just like she was when she first came to view Willow Cottage.

"Would you like a cup of tea before you go?" Holly asked after she'd shown her the house. It's a long drive back to London isn't it?"

"That would be lovely if you could spare the time. Shall I take Ivy?"

"Oh yes please, if you don't mind."

Milly happily held Ivy while Holly made them some tea.

"We're looking for a quick sale," Holly explained as they sipped their tea. "My husband's American and wants us to move to the States. So, it looks like my 'B&B' days are over," she smiled wistfully."

"Did you enjoy doing B&B?"

"I did. It has its ups and its downs but I was at a point when I needed a change in my life and I definitely found it in Willow Cottage."

"Yes, well a change is what I need and fast," Milly smiled, trying to sound upbeat. "I was married for forty years but when my ex-husband died, I discovered that all his assets went to his second wife and their young child.

"Oh, my goodness, that's awful - I am so sorry."

"It's alright dear, she has a young child and so it only seems fair, the law is on their side. Our children have all grown up now."

Doesn't sound fair to me. Married for forty years and she gets nothing? Poor woman

"Well I did get the house, luckily it was in my name."

Thank God for that.

"The trouble is I can't afford to live in it, so when I

was contemplating my future over a quiet brandy in the pub, I picked up a copy of 'Dalton's Weekly' that someone had left and saw your ad selling 'Willow Cottage'."

Images of herself confiding her woes to the lovely taxi driver after that awful night with Mac flashed through Holly's mind.

"Well, as I said Willow Cottage was very lucky for me Mrs Henderson, and so I am sure it could be lucky for you too."
Millie sipped her tea thoughtfully.

"Do you know dear, I have a very strong feeling that you could be right."

END OF BOOK 1

AFTERWORD

My mother Sheila bought Willow Cottage, when she was in her late fifties. A trained nurse, her original plan was to turn it into a residential nursing home.
It was trading as a successful 'Bed and Breakfast' when she bought it and was a favourite with the Goodwood crowd and visiting Americans. They loved the house with its beams and creaky staircases – and often requested a quick tour of the Brewery after hearing all her tales of pirates and ghosts.

Due to health and safety regulations, turning it into a nursing home would have meant the house losing a lot of its charm, and so my mother decided to keep it going as a 'B&B.' Owing to the popularity of the Goodwood racing season and the famous Festival Theatre in Chichester, she also inherited a lot of regular guests from the previous owners, so it seemed silly to 'look a gift horse in the mouth.' Besides which, she was having fun.

She was a stickler for high standards and was very reluctant to let anyone, other than family, run Willow Cottage in her absence. Woe betide us, if there were any stains on the tea-spoons. My brother Stu, did a lot to help her. They were quite a duo.

No spring chicken herself, she ran Willow Cottage as a 'B&B' for thirty odd years while caring for both my grandmother and step-father in their old age.

She had a real life 'Tess,' now buried in a silk-lined coffin with a headstone in the garden. Four other rescue dogs, adopted from the excellent, 'Mount Noddy' re-homing centre near Chichester, kept Tess company. Like Holly, my mother felt a lot safer in the house with her canine companions.

A Vietnamese pot -bellied pig, called Polly, (who features in *'Sunny Side Up'*) lived in the back garden. Another much-loved pet and big hit with visiting children, she was cremated at a pet cemetery in Arundel when she died and there is a little statue of a black pig, commemorating her in the garden.

Guests used to find it very amusing that the owner of a 'B&B," should have a pet pig. My mother always assured them that her beloved pet, wouldn't end up on their plates.

As fun as it was, running a 'B&B' is extremely hard work. You live where you work and work where you live. Your doorbell rings at all times. But life was never dull and my mum met some wonderful people, some of whom became close family friends.

Willow Cottage is a grade 11 listed property, hopefully it will still stand in all its glory welcoming people through its doors for many years to come.

Coming soon

The 'Willow Cottage' Trilogy
Book 2

'Sunny Side Up'

By

CLARE CASSY

Millie Henderson has just turned sixty. Her dream of putting
her feet up and retiring to sunnier climes has been snatched
away and she finds herself having to think about making a
living for the first time in forty years.
Running a B&B is the perfect answer. But she gets a lot more
than she bargains for when she buys Willow Cottage.

By Clare Cassy

TWO OF A KIND

How many chances does one person have to find true love?
When Juanita Estevez' path crosses with Santi Alverez,
a world-famous fashion photographer who rudely snaps a
picture of her when she is out shopping, their worlds are
turned upside down as they come to realise that they are
Two of a Kind.
Both are fiercely ambitious, passionate and supremely
talented at what they do.
But having a talent often has its price.
Can they ever get together and if so, how?

Available on Amazon.com as an eBook or Paperback

Reader Ratings: 4.7 out of 5 Stars

Reviews for Two of a Kind.

Two of a Kind is a happy love story filled with many
unexpected twists and turns. It reminded me a lot of an
international and modern twist on Pride and Prejudice.
The two main characters are incredibly ambitious, and
considering the short timeline within the book (less than a
year for sure), I felt like the character's stories were
developed very well.

***

The book has a very easy-to-follow storyline that many
would enjoy reading while on holiday, or anyone looking for
a brief escape from the mundane aspects of everyday life.
I would recommend this book to anyone looking to
read a cheerful story.

Reviews for Two of a Kind. (cont).

'Every girl's dream, story full of passion, jealousy, travel,
fashion, riches and triumph.
Loved every moment a must read.'

***

Heart-warming with a sense of innocence. A lovely read.

***

Such a lovely and gripping romance between the main
characters. A heart-warming story about following your
dreams and falling in love - and all the bumps along the way.
A fantastic read!

Facebook.com/ClareCassyAuthor

Twitter
@cassy_clare

Printed in Poland
by Amazon Fulfillment
Poland Sp. z o.o., Wrocław